Heroes & Hooligans
Growing Up
In the City
Of Saints

Dennis Ganahl

Heroes & Hooligans
Growing Up in the City of Saints

Text copyright © 2017 by Dennis Ganahl
First Edition
ISBN 978-0-692-86141-7

This book is dedicated to my sons, Denny and Kevin, and all of my family and friends that are such a special part of my life. It's especially dedicated to my dear wife Gina. She gives me the confidence to write my stories and has the patience to listen to them over and over again. She's also a great editor. I love all of you!

Ryan Morris did the graphics and design for the front and back covers. He used the iconic Airway Drive-In sign on the cover. Thanks Ryan!

This book is a humorous historical fiction. My goal is to reconstruct where and how I grew up in St. Ann, Missouri. The places and times are real. The characters and events in my stories aren't real, but I wish they were.

About the Author

There weren't any helicopter parents when I was growing up in St. Ann, Missouri. Our parents, teachers, scoutmasters, and coaches gave us plenty of opportunities to grow up and become independent. As kids, we were given a lot of responsibility and a lot of freedom. Our homes were small and efficient. Everyone was expected to "hold up you're end of the bargain" from a very young age to keep things neat, clean and fixed up.

These stories are my attempt to remember how we grew up, and the many friends I played with in the streets, parks and school playgrounds in St. Louis.

I love to hear and read stories. Missouri is blessed to have such a rich tradition of noted storytellers like Mark Twain, Laura Ingalls Wilder and Walt Disney. Growing up it seemed like all of the adults knew just how to twist or turn a phrase and drop a punch line at just the right moment.

The best storytellers have a way of making you anxious for the story's ending and then making you wish the story were longer.

I hope you enjoy my book and that it makes you wish it were longer.

Dennis Ganahl

Legends in the City of Saints

VIII

x

Chapter 1

Send in the Class Clowns

Why is being good so hard? Mom always says, "Mickey, you better be good," every time I walk out our front door. I try, but it's not easy being good like she wants me to be all of the time. Everyone started teaching me how to walk and how to be good at the same time. With so much practice, you would think I would be as good at one as the other. I'm not.

Now that I'm a big kid in the fourth grade, I'm the fastest kid in my class. Don't you think I'd be the best-behaved kid too? I'm not. Heck I'm not even the second or third best-behaved kid in my class. Why is running so easy to learn and being good so hard to learn? I've been doing both of them the same amount of time.

Heck, Mom says I was running before I was walking to keep up with my older brother Joey. Joey is no saint, but he isn't as fast as me either. It stands to reason that since I'm faster than Joey, I should be better behaved than him too. I'm not. Maybe if I was slower, I'd be better behaved. Doing the right thing is always hard for me especially when I am trying to be good at school.

There are three simple rules to follow to be a good Catholic boy at St. Kevin School. First, obey God; second, obey the stern Dominican nuns; and third, obey your parents. God's rules are simple. Love Him, and treat everyone like you want to be treated. Obeying the nuns and my parents is a lot harder than obeying God because they have a lot more rules than He does.

This afternoon I am supposed to obey my teacher Sister Mary Henry. My class is supposed to walk in two perfectly straight parallel lines without talking or goofing off. Then we have to sit quietly during our school assembly. We are going to see a movie about Jesus' crucifixion. It is supposed to help us prepare for Easter, which is this coming weekend.

What makes this especially tough to do is that Sister Henry does not tell us what to do. She doesn't speak to us in the halls or in church. She is an expert at shepherding us with silent, subtle commando orders like slightly nodding her head, narrowing her eyes, or cocking and twisting her head along with dozens of sharp hand signs and finger snaps. All of her commands are accompanied by her unspoken, but clearly understood threat, "Do what I'm telling you to do immediately or there will be swift and painful punishment."

Today, I am trying my hardest to be good so I won't have to stay after school—again. It is the day before Easter vacation starts and I don't want anything to spoil my days off from school besides our many visits to church for Holy Thursday and Good Friday. My biggest challenge at being good this afternoon is the kid standing in front of me in line. His name is Stubby Brown.

Stubby is the funniest guy alive. Well I take that back. Really Stubby's dad is the funniest guy alive. Stubby is the funniest kid in our school. He is as short and as round as a playground ball. He is a miniature spitting image of 'Curly,' one of the Three Stooges. Stubby can imitate every facial expression, sound effect, joke, and gimmick Curly ever used during the black and white "Captain 11 Showboat," after school TV program.

Whenever I look at Stubby's round Mr. Potato head with his crew cut hair, he starts making goofy faces and sound effects until I can't help but laugh out loud. Stubby is hysterical. He loves to make everybody laugh, and he doesn't stop clowning around until everybody is hooting and hollering or preferably, when somebody wets his pants from laughing so hard.

I knew I was in trouble today, when Stubby butted in front of me on our way to assembly. He immediately started imitating Curly's "Nyuk, Nyuk, Nyuk," laugh while he slapped the top of his head with one hand and waved his other hand back and forth in front of my face acting like he was going to slap me. Not wanting to get in trouble, I knitted my brow, put on my mock-serious angry face and whispered, "Stop goofing off Stubby and turn around or I will tell Sister Henry!"

What a mistake. My threat merely served as a dare to Stubby. He redoubled his efforts to make me laugh out loud as we strode down the highly polished hallway. At the front of our line, marched Sister Henry. She looked straight ahead and stood as straight as the yardstick she carried around our classroom. She was leading us toward the school assembly in two single file lines. The left line was for the girls in our class and the right line was for the boys. All of the other classes were in the same type of lines.

As we marched in unison, Sister Henry would spin her head around with breakneck speed in an attempt to catch one of us doing something behind her back. Sister Henry could swivel her head 180 degrees without moving her shoulders one quarter of an inch, just like an owl. We all knew Stubby had "nun radar." Every time Sister's head spun around like a snowy barn owl, Stubby would be facing forward with a mock serious smirk on his face. Then, the instant Sister faced forward again reassured that we were behaving; Stubby would whirl around with his eyes crossed and his hand slapping the top of his head, trying to get me to laugh.

Stubby's timing was flawless until our class came to an intersection of hallways. As we did, Sister Henry sharply raised her open right hand toward heaven, which meant 'stop—immediately.'

Stubby's nun-radar failed. He was walking backwards facing towards me, when everybody stopped—immediately, except Stubby. He set off a stupefying sequence of astonishing actions and reactions that unfolded in slow motion right before my very eyes.

While walking backwards with his crazed eyes wide open, Stubby's round playground ball body rammed hard into Donnie's back. This caused Donnie to gasp and throw his open hands towards heaven, as his head slammed hard into Tommy's back. Tommy gasped, threw his open hands towards heaven and plowed into Larry. Larry cried out, threw his open hands towards heaven, and clunked skulls with Jimmy, who grunted and wheezed as his body flew headlong into a gasping Mike. Mike valiantly tried to stop himself from careening headlong into the pit of Sister Henry's back. He failed.

Mike slammed hard into the always erect-standing Sister Henry, who still had her right hand pointing straight toward heaven. Sister was toppled like a tall and mighty oak. The kid who got the worst of it was the one that Sister Henry smashed, Timmy Meeks. Everyone had fallen like a line of domino tiles.

Timmy was pressed like the maple leaf in our classroom's Oxford English dictionary. All of the air in Timmy's lungs escaped in one huge wheeze that sounded like a popped brown paper lunch bag. We all heard him groan, "Uuuuuuugggggggggghhhhhhhh," as he was ground into the highly polished maroon and black tile floor. I figured Timmy was dead or at least unconscious.

As everyone lay sprawled out on the floor, it took a moment for the rest of us to recognize which arms and legs were connected to whose head and body. Sister was sprawled face down. I could barely see Timmy's hands and feet. He looked like a swatted fly. His small hands and feet could barely be seen as they stretched out from under Sister's elaborate black and white habit.

Everything happened so quickly I didn't take time to think before I blurted out, "Hey, Stubby, you got a strike!" Worse, I didn't realize that anyone had heard me until everybody, except Sister Henry and Timmy, erupted into hysterical laughter with tears running down their cheeks.

Stubby was lying on his back like a turtle staring up at me on top of a laughing and moaning Donnie. The harder Stubby laughed the more he rolled on the ground, holding his chuckling stomach until finally—Stubby wet his pants and the wet spot just kept growing.

The only blood I saw came from Larry's nose, but Sister Henry's pride was badly bruised, and she almost seemed to levitate as she arose straight as a pencil, while she straightened her habit. When she turned to face us, her face was the color of Hell's fires. She put her hands on her hips and stared down her long, pointy nose at Stubby and me. She was ready to mete out justice and I wished I were dead. The rest of the guys painfully picked themselves up off of the floor.

Slowly Sister growled, "Misters McBride and Brown get out of line—right now." She pointed at the wall and pulled her handkerchief from somewhere up her sleeve as she handed it to Larry for his bleeding nose without looking at him.

"Everyone BE QUIET and get in line," she commanded in her steely voice as she put her long index finger to her lips to signal us to keep quiet. Then she narrowed her eyes and focused her x-ray laser vision on Stubby and me until her eyes burned holes into my quivering soul. Stubby just shrugged.

Everyone became quiet as church mice and they jumped back into their lines. No one dared look at Stubby or me—we were the unclean, the sinners. Cautiously, Stubby and I stepped out of line. I stood with the hangdog look of a condemned man backed against the beige concrete cinderblock wall. I was afraid to look at Stubby. He was probably smiling.

Silently, Sister floated over to us with her hands on her hips and the look of cold contempt. As she looked down at the wet spot on Stubby's pants her face convulsed into a twisted red mask of rage. Repulsed, she slowly shook her head from side to side as an unholy smile crossed her snarled lips.

"Tsk, tsk, tsk! Look at yourself Mr. Brown. You're disgusting," she snarled as she slowly eyed him up and down.

And without batting an eye and sounding very genuine, Stubby sweetly said, "Thank you Sister Mary Henry."

"I didn't mean it as a compliment you urchin," she hissed, "Go to the principal's office right now. Have them call your parents so they can pick you up and take you home," Sister commanded pointing her long, straight right index finger toward the principal's office.

"Thank you Sister," Stubby happily said over his shoulder as he kind of skipped down the hall. Sister's look of cold contempt didn't change as she thwacked me hard on the right side of my head with the simple gold wedding band that she wore to symbolize her commitment to God. A Dominican nun knows exactly how to get your attention. Ultimately everyone, except hardened criminals like Stubby give up.

"Mickey, you will keep me company for the rest of the day. Stay right next to me so that I remember you're going to stay after school to clean our chalkboards."

"Yes, Sister," I whimpered as I reminded myself to never stand next to Stubby again.

As I looked down the hall, I saw Stubby give his 'Curly shuffle' right before he skipped into the principal's office. It showed me once again that the harder I tried to be good the quicker I got punished for being bad. It all seemed so unfair. Stubby knocked everybody down because he was goofing off and escaped because he wet his pants. All I did was accidently tell a joke.

After my classmates were in straight lines, one head behind the other, we marched into the cafeteria with Sister Henry leading us just like the rest of the classes. The girls sat on the left side of the cafeteria and the boys sat on the right side for the school assembly.

In organized Catholic fashion, the youngest kids were seated in the front rows and the eighth graders were seated in the back rows, so everyone could see.

This meant my fourth grade class was sitting right in the middle of the cafeteria. I was sitting on the center aisle metal folding chair in front of Sister Henry right next to the movie projector. I could see everyone really good. The film projector was sitting on top of one of the church's wooden collection boxes. The collection box and the projector were stacked on top of a folding cafeteria table that was set in the center aisle. There was also a folding chair set on the table for the projectionist, but no one was sitting in it.

Slowly, I craned my head around trying to find my older brother Joey, who is in sixth grade. The cafeteria was filling up quickly with freshly scrubbed girls dressed in green, blue and red plaid uniforms with white blouses and boys dressed in collared shirts, dress pants, and dress shoes.

Impatiently, we all sat and waited for everyone to be seated. All of the kids, except me, were whispering their plans for their Easter vacation. I was trying to act good so that Sister would give me time off after school for good behavior. The kids' whispers were creating a low rumbling buzz that was causing the nuns to feel frenzied and out of control. The buzzing was sending the nuns into a whirl of motion causing a blur of black and white, as they worked to get everyone quiet.

Joey walked into the cafeteria, and our eyes met immediately. We smiled. Once I knew my brother was here and okay, I watched some of the eighth grade boys plug the wires and string the film through the projector at the directions of Mr. Stewart.

9

All of the other boys were envious of the eighth grade boys. Eighth graders were the luckiest guys in school. Every day they got out of class earlier than us to be crossing guards, and hall and cafeteria monitors, when the rest of us were still in our classrooms. They also got to leave class to set up or take down the metal folding chairs for assemblies, church services, lunches or any other special occasion.

Mr. Stewart was the only man we saw in St. Kevin during the day except for our pastor Father Christiansen and his assistant pastor Father Cross. Mr. Stewart was a kindly man, who wore a very clean white T-shirt, a black leather belt, gray work pants, white cotton socks, and black leather shoes everyday. His dark but thinning hair was always neatly combed straight back and he was always smiling, even when he was mopping up some kid's puke or pee. I never heard him yell at a kid even if they had broken a window, like I did once. He was always busy doing chores like washing windows, mopping and buffing floors, changing light bulbs, and fixing stuff around school.

Everyone's favorite nun, Sister Mary Karen always said, "Now class, everyone say thank you to Mr. Stewart for being St. Kevin's guardian angel. I simply don't know what we'd do without him." And in unison we'd sing, " Thank you Mr. Stewart!" and he'd humbly reply, "You're welcome class."

As I rubbernecked around the cafeteria, I winced as I saw Sister Mary Regina slap a fifth-grade boy across the face. After she slapped him, she grabbed him by the ear and marched him towards three other repentant looking boys from her class. They were all kneeling on the hard tile floor facing the wall. Immediately, I said a silent prayer that she wouldn't be my teacher next year.

In passing, I saw some eighth grade boys whispering and snickering to each other like they had just heard the best joke ever told. None of them could hold a straight face. They were ganged up in the very back part of the cafeteria with their arms folded trying not to look suspicious. Smack dab in the middle of the eighth grade gang stood Sonny. Sonny always looked like he was snarling even when he laughed. He was the biggest hell raiser in our school, and he was always in Sister Mary George's principal office. Everyone joked that he was in her office so often that he should have his own desk.

Sonny and Sister Mary George were locked in a battle of unnatural wills. She was determined to save his soul and he was determined to burn in Hell. Their battles raged daily and I'm sure she prayed nightly for his salvation.

He would break one, or more, of her golden rules and she would break one, or more, of her wooden rulers on some part of his body everyday. Their battles provided daily drama. Everybody that walked past Sister's office always peeked inside just to see if Sonny was there—yet.

Many people thought Sonny was evil. He greased his hair, smoked cigarettes and hung out on the corner saying sassy stuff to everybody, but he never sassed his mom. He was the best athlete in eighth grade, but Sister George would not let him play on any school teams because of his poor behavior and conduct. He didn't care a bit. Sonny only obeyed his dad. His dad's name was Stanley Boxer, and Sonny's God-given name was Stanley Boxer Junior, but woe to the person that ever called him anything but Sonny. His dad called him, 'Sonny-Boy.'

Sister Mary George reminded me of my neighbor's Boston terrier because her Dominican habit was black and white, and she was shorter than most of the fourth graders. Her face had jowls and they were always in a snarl. She always had her chrome whistle handy as it hung from her black leather belt. She blew it so loudly that your ears would ring for half an hour afterwards, if you were anywhere near her, when she let go with a shrill blast, which she did regularly both inside and outside of the school buildings.

Once all of the students were seated and the film was threaded into the projector, Mr. Stewart instructed the boys, how to flip the "ON" switch. Then Mr. Stewart left the cafeteria and headed toward the boiler room, which served as his office. Seeing the kids seated and Mr. Stewart leave, Sister George walked briskly towards the back of the cafeteria, which was where the movie screen was hung on the tall brick wall. Sister was so short, you could barely see the top of her black hood, as she stood in front of the whole school. She expected everyone to automatically be quiet, but we were too excited. The eighth graders had built a make-do stage out of folding tables and chairs, which looked pretty rickety, but Sister must have thought it was safe.

To get our attention, she stepped up onto the seat of the metal folding chair that was placed as a stair to the cafeteria-table stage. As she inspected the wobbly table, she decided not to climb up. Instead she just stood on the chair. Standing on the chair, we could still only barely see the top of the hood of her habit. She put her index finger to her lips, but everyone kept talking because they couldn't see her.

Frustrated and evidently feeling safe in the hands of the Lord, Sister exhaled a deep breath, and carefully stepped from the seat of the folding metal chair onto the top of the cafeteria table, which wobbled as she nervously stood in the middle of it, not wanting to move again. She was trying to keep her balance and quietly get everyone's attention. Now, everyone saw her entire body precariously perched on top of the table, but they still kept talking. In final desperation, Sister pulled out her chrome-plated police whistle and let go with three shrill blasts, "TWWWWEEEEEEEEEEEEEET!

"TWWWWEEEEEEEEEEEEEET!

"TWWWWEEEEEEEEEEEEEET!" the shrill echoes reverberated throughout the concrete block cafeteria for a solid minute. When the echoes stopped, our ears were ringing, and you better believe Sister Mary George had our rapt attention. The other sisters folded their arms and silently nodded their approval as the students sat mute, and deaf.

"Good afternoon students, may God bless you!" said Sister George.

"Good afternoon Sister, may God bless you!" we sang in chorus-like fashion in response.

"Is everyone ready for a blessed Easter vacation?" asked Sister George.

13

"Yes, Sister," we sang back. "

"Well that's just fine," said Sister. " We have a wonderful movie to watch this afternoon. Do you like to watch movies children?" asked Sister. "Yes, Sister!" we sang.

"Excellent. This movie is very special; it's about Jesus' last days before He died on the cross and was resurrected. Does anyone know why Jesus let Himself be nailed on the cross?" asked Sister as I winced thinking about it.

Most of the kids sitting up front were frantic to answer her question. They were half-standing and half-sitting in their chairs with their hands waving wildly, saying, "Call on me Sister, call on me!" or "Me, me, me, Sister!"

Finally Sister George selected a little boy up front and said, "Can you tell me Mr. Jordan?"

"Yes I can Sister because Jesus loves us," said young Phillip Jordan.

"That's very good Mr. Jordan, Jesus does love us very much. How about you Miss Wise, can you help us?"

"Yes Sister. Jesus died on the cross so that we are forgiven for our Original Sin and so we can go to heaven and be with Him for eternity," said young Miss Wise.

"Well, I'm very impressed with your answer Miss Wise, come to my office after school and I will give you a special treat, thank you!' said Sister George.

With a look of extreme satisfaction on her face, Sister George proudly put her hands on her hips, as the table wobbled unsteadily, and said; "Now students, we're going to start the movie. It runs about one hour. After the movie, remain seated and be quiet. If you are well behaved during and after the movie, I will dismiss you from the cafeteria for your Easter vacation."

And with that everyone gave a great roar of approval and cheers. Then Sister smiled and raised her hand to signal for quiet and she got it—immediately.

"Okay, Mr. Carpenter (Leo Carpenter was the lucky-dog-eighth-grader who got to start the movie), would you please start the movie?" And, with that Sister very carefully clambered off the table, and landed onto the metal folding chair, where she stopped for just a second to catch her breath. Then she stepped off of the chair onto the highly polished floor and marched with her head held high toward the hall exit.

Over the exit doorway was a wooden sign with an inscription painted in black Old English letters that said, "A Family that Prays Together, Stays Together." As Sister marched out of the cafeteria someone turned out the lights.

For the few seconds while it was dark, some of the kids gave catcalls or imitated scary sound effects as the nuns scurried around slapping the heads of the boys closest to them. After Leo turned on the projector, he walked to the back of the cafeteria with the other eighth grade boys.

The projector came to life and started clicking and ticking as the film wound through all of its metal sprockets between the two huge spinning metal reels, one emptying while the other began to fill up.

15

All of the dark shades on the windows had been pulled down and black drapes had been hung over the outside glass doors. In a few moments my eyes adjusted to the darkness. I could easily see the lit screen because the bright light from the projector was the only light in the room, except the red exit lights. As I listened to the projector whir, I watched numbers on the screen countdown backwards starting with 10-9-8-7-6-5-4-3-2-1 and then the movie started.

How the black and white movie about Jesus' life started was confusing to me and I am guessing to everybody else too. It opened with a dark-haired woman with a very big smile. She was sitting in a wingback chair that you would see in any living room looking straight out at the audience. She looked like any of our mothers. She was wearing a modern collared dress, with white polka dots and a pearl necklace. She was dressed like she was going to church. A cute baby was sitting in her lap. The baby was "Goo-gooing and gaaahh-gaaahhing" into the camera. The sight of the smiling mother holding her baby caused most of the girls in the audience to exclaim a big loud, "ooooooooohh and aaaahhhh, isn't the baby cute!" response.

Then I heard this loud and ominous laugh that sounded like a combination of coughs and machine gun bullets ring out from the darkness in the back of the cafeteria, "Ha-Ha-Ha-Ha-Ha-Ha-Ha-Ha!" The loud evil laugh sounded scary and unnerving.

Next, the pretty young mother on the screen laid her baby across her lap and said, "Babies are a very special gift from God, and we need to nurture their souls, their minds and their bodies."

Again, I heard that loud, evil laugh from the darkness.

Soon, the mother unbuttoned the top of her dress, and began to breast feed her baby. Although it was dark, I'm pretty sure everybody's face in the cafeteria was glowing brighter red than any of the exit signs. My cheeks, and I am pretty sure my soul was burning as I watched the woman in complete disbelief at what I was seeing. As the baby suckled, large white words appeared on the screen, "Catholic Series on Motherhood: How to Breastfeed Your Baby," I said a quick prayer that the words would disappear fast, so I could see again, and they did.

Again, I heard that loud, evil ominous laugh from the darkness, "Ha-Ha-Ha-Ha-Ha!"

Everyone was sitting absolutely still with their mouths wide open. They were shocked and stunned by what they were watching. Although it seemed like the movie had been running for an hour, within a minute all of the nuns were buzzing like bees and I heard Sister Henry yell to us, "Don't look at that movie. Look away," but I didn't plan to quit looking and I am sure none of my friends did either.

All of the sudden out of nowhere, a frantic Sister George came charging back into the cafeteria. She was running so fast, she was a blur, as she waved her hands and yelled and screamed indiscernible commands. She headed for the rickety table and chair stage. Again, I heard that loud, evil laugh from the darkness, "Ha-Ha-Ha-Ha-Ha!"

When Sister George, arrived at the makeshift stage, she didn't pause to think about her safety. She leapt on to the metal folding chair with total faith that it wouldn't buckle and knock her to the ground. Her faith was rewarded; the chair didn't crash to the floor. Then with the same faith, she leapt onto the cafeteria table believing it too would hold and through the grace of God, it did.

Although the table was pretty wobbly, Sister stood up straight looking totally surprised at what she had just accomplished. Once she was on top of the table, a look of triumph crept over her face and I understood her plan. She intended to stand in the center of the stage, and wave her arms to block the movie picture with her body until someone turned off the projector. As she haltingly scooted to the center of the stage, she commanded at the top of her lungs, "Turn off the projector! Turn off the projector!" Then Sister began blowing her police whistle as loud as humanly possible so we couldn't hear what the woman on the screen was saying. Sister George looked like a white ghost as the light from the projector reflected onto her white habit.

"TWWWWEEEEEEEEEEEEET!

"TWWWWEEEEEEEEEEEEET!

"TWWWWEEEEEEEEEEEEET!" At one point, her whistle became so shrill only dogs could have heard it.

The one thing Sister George didn't plan on was the fact that her habit was white and that was the same color as the movie screen. So, instead of blocking the movie, the movie was projected onto her habit and Sister's face became part of the macabre scene unfolding before our disbelieving eyes. Sister's face was actually superimposed over the baby's face. It was a surreal moment. Sister stood in the center of the stage, wildly waving her arms, and loudly blowing her whistle, while we watched the mother breast feed her. All 500 grade school kids were so stunned that we sat as quiet as if we were at Mass.

The only sound louder than Sister's whistle was the loud devilish laughter buried deep in the darkness of the cafeteria. The laughter ratta-tat-tatted louder and longer as the projector clicked through more and more frames of the movie, "Ha-Ha-Ha-Ha-Ha-Ha-Ha-Ha-Ha-Ha!!"

I don't know what spirit possessed me, but I suddenly leaped out of my metal folding chair and pulled the plug to the long extension cord, which snaked from the movie projector through the cafeteria to an outlet in the concrete block wall. The movie, which bewitched everyone, took the appearance of dying animal as its sound and picture slowly whirred to an abrupt stop with the mother in mid-sentence. Like Michael the Archangel, I proudly stood holding the vanquished and harmless extension cord high above my head and pointed it toward heaven.

In the darkness, you could barely see Sister George still wildly waving her hands towards heaven and blasting away on her whistle, when she finally realized her students were no longer under siege by the devil. Someone turned on the lights. Looking thoroughly exhausted and emotionally spent, Sister exclaimed loud enough for everyone to hear, "Thank you Mr. McBride,' and then she heaved a big sigh and gave an approving smile, marking me as a hero.

I am not sure why I pulled the projector's plug. It just seemed like the right thing to do, especially with Sister George looking so desperate as she stood on the quaking and creaking cafeteria table.

The entire school was released early, and Sister Henry forgave my after school detention. As I walked out of the cafeteria door, I felt pretty darn good about pulling the plug until my buddies started razzing me. They wanted to watch more of the movie, and honestly I did too. My status as school hero was over, when Sonny and his gang found me outside. One by one each guy knocked into me and mumbled something to me.

"You baby, you ruined it for everybody. Are you afraid of movies?"

"Way to go Mickey, you ruined the joke!"

"Real smart Sherlock!"

"You brown-noser."

"Loser!

Sonny didn't say or do anything to me. He just stood there staring at me with a smug smirk as my older brother Joey came up and said, "Come on Mickey, let's go home."

Nervous, I followed as Joey led me away from Sonny and his hooligan buddies. As we hurried away, I heard that snide ratta-tat Tommy gun laugh I had heard during the movie.

That is the weird thing about being good. When you try to be good you aren't and when you don't try to be good you are. Go figure.

Chapter 2

Greatest Easter Egg Hunt Story Ever Told

St. Ann is a Catholic Mecca and you can always find lots of Catholic kids and a convenient Mass. It is 1963 and my family is living the American dream in what's called an affordable, stick-built, post-war house in a city named St. Ann on a street named St. Stephen Lane.

All of the streets in St. Ann and most of the people are named after Catholic saints. A list of my friends' names read like the Litany of Saints, Joey, Tommy, Mike, Johnny, Dave, Andy, Larry, Phil, Jimmy, Paul, Kevin, Denny and Pete.

I was very young when I learned that St. Stephen was the first Catholic martyr and that if I didn't behave myself I could end up being a martyr too. Almost everyone I know is a Catholic or a Christian of some sort like Protestant, Methodist, or Lutheran. I'm not sure what the differences are between Catholics and all of the other Christian religions. Most of the Catholic kids go to Catholic grade schools but we play with the kids that don't go to Catholic schools after school on the weekends and during the summer.

We Catholic families usually have more than the national average of two and a half kids. My family has two kids, but we are a small Catholic family. It isn't uncommon for Catholic families to have four or five kids; eight kids are a lot even by Catholic standards. It is a challenge to live in a place with streets named after holy people like saints. I always feel a lot of pressure to be good and a lot of pressure to be bad because I don't want to be a kiss-up or a goody-two-shoes all of the time; it is the age-old Abel versus Cain battle.

Our small home in St. Ann is a lot nicer and bigger than our first home which was a rented apartment in a five-family flat on Shenandoah Street in south St. Louis city. Our old apartment only had one bedroom for all four of us. In St. Ann, we are blessed. We have a little heaven on earth.

We are buying our home. It has two small bedrooms for four people, a modern kitchen with white gleaming metal cabinets, an electric dishwasher, and a washing machine and dryer. Our full concrete basement is dry, our backyard is fenced, and we have our choice of

Catholic churches like St. Kevin, St. Gregory, St. William or St. Mary to attend Mass. We could've gone to St. Ann School, which is a good public school with a lot of my friends, but we go to St. Kevin's Catholic Church and School. Imagine, even our public grade school is named after a saint.

I feel a little guilty because I don't like Easter as well as Christmas. The nuns tell us that Easter is every Catholic's most important religious holiday because it guarantees us the possibility of eternal salvation. I guess the nuns never had a room full of brightly wrapped presents under a lighted Christmas tree and two weeks off to play with them. If they did, they would like Christmas better than Easter too. To a kid like me, eternal salvation doesn't seem all that important in the big scheme of things.

Easter is my second favorite holiday for two reasons. One, I like Christmas presents better than Easter candy, and two, I get more days off from school for Christmas than for Easter. That said, the first-ever *"St. Kevin's Knights of Columbus Easter Egg Hunt"* had me rethinking my holiday priorities. The Knights are giving away a cool red Schwinn racer if you can find their hidden golden egg.

To my Mom, eternal salvation means everything and she wants to make sure we are dressed for the occasion. Our new Easter Sunday clothes are our sign of soulful renewal, just like spring starts a new year after a long, cold winter. We have been shopping for Easter Sunday church clothes since Christmas. We've shopped at Stix, Baer & Fuller, Boyd's, and the Famous-Barr stores in downtown St. Louis, and the Robert Hall store in St. Ann. We have also been trying on shoes at every Buster Brown and Boyd's store between the Mississippi and Missouri rivers.

Mom's responsibility is fashion and style and she is determined to find the best looking togs available. She wants our family looking picture perfect for church and the Easter photos of us holding our Easter baskets. Besides fashionable, our Easter Sunday clothes have to be sturdy. They are going to be worn to every Sunday Mass, holiday, special occasion and family birthday dinner until next Easter. How much our new clothes cost is of little concern to Mom, that's Dad's job.

Dad's responsibilities for our clothes are size, construction and cost. He makes sure the clothes Mom selects are large enough to be worn for a full year and sturdy enough to be passed down to the next kid in line and it doesn't matter whose family wears them. Clothes are always useful and never simply thrown away. Cost is important because Dad pays "cash on the barrelhead." Our family doesn't use our Diner credit card nor does any other family we know. So, if the outfit Mom selects doesn't get Dad's financial approval changes are expected, but Mom can be very persuasive and Dad can't match her shopping stamina. She usually wins the battle of wills.

This Easter is a big one for me. I don't have to wear Joey's or my cousins' hand-me-down Sunday clothes like I always have before. In the past, all I got to buy was new shoes, underwear and socks. I wore everybody else's sport coats, slacks, ties and belts, which was good in one way. My wardrobe had selection. Where Joey only had one sport coat that fit, I had several choices that may or may not fit. This year Mom says I am too old to wear anyone's hand-me-downs.

After the months long clothing ordeal, it is decided that I will wear a camel colored sport jacket, yellow button-down oxford shirt, and a burgundy and gold clip-on tie. After begging over several trips to the local Robert Hall store, Mom relented, and bought me the coolest pair of olive colored sharkskin pants I have ever seen. They look iridescent-gold in the sunshine. The pants look great with my oxblood-colored, pebble-grained Winthrop shoes that have steel taps. Dad said everything was too expensive, but it didn't matter in the end as he reluctantly wrote a personal check.

Getting taps on the heels of my shoes is a big step to being grown up. All of the older guys who are cool have taps on their dress shoes. When a guy walks with taps on tile and wooden floors or heck even outside on the concrete he is making a statement.

He is saying, "I am HERE and I am *COOL*. HEAR ME. SEE ME."

Parents don't like the sound taps make, but they do like the fact that taps stop the heels of their kids' shoes from wearing down too quickly. A tap is a lot cheaper than replacing a shoe's rubber or leather heel.

There was a big difference between the size and style of taps guys had the shoe repairman nail onto their shoes. Mine were smaller 'quarter-moon' steel taps. Hoods and greasers wore a steel 'horseshoe' taps that covered the entire heel of their shoe just like a tap dancer. When they clomped along on tile floors, their shoes clipped-clopped so loudly they couldn't hear the nuns telling them what to do. For that reason, horseshoe taps were banned in St. Kevin's buildings and hallways, but on the weekends and after school, the hoods and greasers wore them on their black shoes with white socks and blue jeans. Some fathers had small steel wedged cleats that made a duller thud sound in their shoes' heals.

The night before Easter, after we dyed our hard-boiled Easter eggs, I laid my new Easter clothes out to wear to church in the morning. Then I shined my miraculous medal, kissed my parents good night and went to bed, where I had a chance to tell Joey my closely held secret.

"Guess what Joey. I am going to win the brand new, red Schwinn racer tomorrow at the Easter Egg Hunt."

"Yeah, you and every other kid. What makes you think you are going to win it, Mickey?"

"Well, I am the fastest kid in the neighborhood, ain't I?"

"Yeah but there are a lot of guys bigger than you, so don't count on winning—now go to sleep before Dad hears us, good night!" With that he abruptly turned over on his stomach and went to sleep, while I lay there fuming and thinking about why Joey would be so mean to me.

In the end, all he did was make me even more sure that I was going to find the golden egg and win that brand new red Schwinn racer tomorrow. If I didn't win the red racer what was I supposed to ride all summer the "Black Beast?"

Joey didn't need a new bike: he already had a sleek, black Schwinn racer. He got it, when he turned 10 years old. I'm not turning 10 until next fall; I have a whole summer in between.

Once Joey got his Schwinn, I couldn't keep up with him on my little kid bike anymore, and I would be behind him two blocks chasing and screaming for him to "wait up."

In those days, my legs were too short. I couldn't ride his 26-inch bike without "racking" myself on the crossbar. When our neighbor Frank saw me chasing after Joey one day, he gave me his daughter's old pink and white hand-me-down bike, which didn't have a crossbar. Frannie had quit riding her bike, when she became a teenager because it wasn't "cool" for older kids to ride bikes. I wouldn't ride the pink and white bike either, so Frank and Dad took it apart and painted its frame and wheels black to make it look "cool." But in the end, no matter what color it was painted, it was still a girl's bike, and I got a lot of grief from the guys, when I rode it. I called it the 'Black Beast' so it sounded like a super hero.

The Black Beast had fat balloon tires and a big, leather saddle seat with springs as long as bananas, but its best feature was its 26-inch wheels. On it, I could keep up with Joey and his friends without racking myself. The Black Beast was different and everybody thought I "looked cute" riding it.

The Star community newspaper even published my photograph riding it during the 1960 presidential election. I decorated it with lots of John Kennedy's bumper stickers, yard signs, and red, white and blue bunting for a July Fourth parade. I wasn't a member of any political party, but I was Catholic and so was Kennedy. The only problem with the Beast was that my legs were so short I couldn't sit on its seat and peddle at the same time. That worked out great for Dave, one of my best friends.

Dave lived four houses away from me, and he was the youngest of eight kids—seven brothers and one sister. His sister was the oldest kid and she was real bossy, so it was like having two mothers. Dave didn't have a bike. He had lots of hand-me-down stuff, but he didn't get things handed down to him, he got parts of things handed down to him. Everything was either broken or worn out by the time it got to Dave. Having all of those parts was really good for building stuff.

Take Dave's wagon wheels. He didn't have a wagon, but he did have four wheels from two different wagons. The wagon wheels were great for building wooden hot rods that we pushed down hilly streets and the W.T. Grant parking lot. It worked great having two larger wheels in the back and two smaller wheels in the front of the hot rod. Dave even had a steering wheel to steer our hot rods. Of course he didn't have a real car.

His family did have several bike frames, and five different sized bike wheels, but he didn't have tires or inner tubes for any of the bike wheels, and of course he didn't have enough money to buy them either.

So, Dave would sit on the Black Beast's seat and put his hands on my shoulders for balance while I peddled and steered. We would switch places, when I needed to rest while we were coasting. Making the switch was pretty tricky to do without crashing. After we would switch positions, Dave would peddle while I rested in the Black Beast's seat. We were a great team.

One day, Dave got bored riding on the Beast's seat so he invented street skiing. His idea was to roller skate behind the Beast with a rope tied around its seat so the skater could be pulled behind the bike just like a water skier. It was a great idea. We found two different skates to use in his basement. One was a leather boot and the other was a metal skate that clamped onto hard-soled leather shoes. The skates worked okay and since it was Dave's idea he tried it first.

I grunted through the first couple of pedals to take off towing Dave. His weight pulled me backward, but before I knew it, we were off and Dave was skiing in the street behind me just like he envisioned. I watched out for potholes, waves and tar humps that melted and got sticky during the hottest summer days. We called it "freewheeling."

We were naturals, but we did have our share of skin-scraping headlong dives into the street, when we tried jumping the curbs. Everything about freewheeling except the bruises, scrapes, and spilled blood was a blast. Luckily, nobody lost any teeth or broke any bones.

Yeah, I would miss the Black Beast, but I was determined to win that brand new red Schwinn at the

"First Annual Knights of Columbus Easter Egg Hunt." As I was about to fall sleep, my last thought was to give Dave the Beast, when I won the red Schwinn. I was going to nickname my new red Schwinn, 'The Rocket.'

Easter Sunday morning was beautiful and pretty warm. Joey and I woke up first. It was about six o'clock in the morning, and our parents followed us groggily around the house as we looked for decorated hardboiled eggs and candy to put into our Easter baskets. We searched and searched until we thought we found every piece of candy that had been hidden. One year, I found one chocolate bunny that had actually turned white it was so old, but it still tasted pretty good. Just like every year before, I planned to eat as much Easter candy as I could before I was told to stop. So, I ate for all of my worth until it was time to get ready for church.

We went to Mass every Sunday, so you better believe we were early for Mass on Easter even though Dad was taking photos before we left for church. To complete our Easter ensembles, Dad had bought Mom a spring flower corsage and Joey, Dad and me had white carnation boutonnières pinned to the lapels of our sport coats.

Since Joey was an altar boy for Mass, Dad took pictures of him with his altar boy's vestments and his Easter clothes. Joey knew the whole Mass in Latin. I could only repeat a few of the Latin phrases, so I read the English version in my Missal. The whole time Dad was taking pictures of Joey, I was kidding Joey about being on the cover of *Life* magazine.

As we walked into St. Kevin church for the 10 a.m. Mass, I could smell the heavy incense from the earlier Masses. Everyone in church was dressed in his or her best Sunday clothes. Mothers wore very colorful, stylish and elaborate hats. The daughters all wore veils of various styles and designs. The younger girls wore white veils from the First Communion, and many of their older sisters wore the fashionable and elaborate black veils.

St. Kevin was a great place to watch my friends and their families, and on Easter Sunday the girls were especially pretty and everyone was smiling brightly at the prospect of eternal salvation. As the families marched into church, we had our own Easter parade, as a continuous procession of people politely promenaded into and out of church displaying their Easter finery and good manners.

After Mass, on our way out of church, everyone shook Father Christiansen's hand and smiled and waved to other families and friends and wished them, "Happy Easter!"

Sunday breakfasts were the only meals Dad cooked and Easter was no exception. He pulled out his heavy 12-inch iron skillet and fried the thick sliced fatty bacon first. Next, he fried our eggs in the bacon grease. Joey and I toasted the bread, set the table and poured the orange juice into recycled jelly jars with pictures of cartoon characters and Davy Crocket mugs. Mom poured the black, hot Folgers coffee for her and Dad. She kept all of the empty coffee cans for bacon grease or old nails and screws that Dad kept on his workbench.

Everyone got two slices of bacon and one sunny-side-up and well-peppered egg. The bacon and eggs were served with as many slices of buttered white toast and jelly as you could eat. Breakfast was ready when we all sat down to eat together. It was a rare treat, when Dad accidentally broke your egg yolk. You were allowed to make it into an egg sandwich using the buttered and jelly toast. Like all of the other meals in our home, you didn't fill up on the entrée. That is why lots of white bread was always on the table.

Easter breakfast was always special because I got to eat candy along with my regular breakfast, and I got a decorated hard-boiled egg too. By the end of breakfast, I was full so I asked to be excused from the table.

"What's your hurry Mickey?" asked Dad.

I quickly explained my plan to win the red Schwinn racer and asked if I could get Dave and go to the Knights of Columbus Easter Egg Hunt. He said, "Okay, but...DON'T forget to change your church clothes."

"Yes sir!" I said over my shoulder as I ran to my room. Hearing Dad, Mom added, "Wear your nice jeans Mickey. Don't wear any with holes in the knees and wear a school shirt not a T-shirt."

The nice jeans were okay with me but I didn't want to wear a school shirt to the egg hunt so I bargained with her. "It's a little chilly," I said, "can I wear a sweatshirt instead?"

"Okay, as long as it's not a ratty looking one," she replied.

In the past, it has been an argument at my house about wearing our Easter clothes all day after church.

Mom thought we should until last year when everything changed. Joey, Uncle Paul and I knocked the knees out of our wool dress pants playing basketball at St. Ann Park. We would've gotten punished for days if Grandma hadn't told Mom that she was silly expecting us to stay dressed up all day.

"They're just being boys, what do you expect? Let them change into their play clothes after church, the Lord won't be upset." And that was that. When Grandma told Mom to do something, Mom did it, no questions asked. Once a parent gets a hold on their kid, it is almost impossible to shake them off. When you agree parents are the bosses, they are—or think they are—forever.

Picking out my play clothes was a lot different than picking out Easter clothes. My blue jeans fell into one of three categories: newer, patched, and beyond repair, which were cut off into shorts. I had an older brother and two older cousins that were bigger than me so I had a large wardrobe.

Together those guys had given me enough pants to wear until I got married. All of my blue jeans were patched, hand-me downs, just like my bike. Some had been worn by all four of us. The knees got ripped out of the jeans because we crawled on the ground, climbed trees, slid into bases, fell off our bikes, cut the grass, and played in the creek. We did anything that we could imagine when we played. If the jeans were too big for me Mom washed them in hot water to shrink them and I rolled-up the cuffs and cinched them tight with my brother's old belt. Once my jeans became completely worn out Mom would cut off the legs for shorts or cut them into patches for when my newer jeans got holes in them.

Blue jeans went with everything in my wardrobe, especially my white T-shirts, sweatshirts, and high-top or low-top 'tennis shoes.' I would usually get a pair of black high top tennis shoes in the fall and white low top tennis shoes in the summer. It did not matter if they were Keds, Converse or P.F. Flyers as long as they were on sale. We wore the same pair of tennis shoes everywhere except church and school until they literally fell off our feet completely worn out with holes everywhere. Dad hadn't figured out anyway to recycle them like he did our bike's inner tubes, which were cut up into rubber bands and stored in a recycled one-pound Folgers' steel coffee can.

When Dave and I arrived at the park on the Black Beast, there was a colorful banner stretched across Ashby Road that proclaimed, "Knights of Columbus Easter Egg Hunt." We were blown away at how many families with kids had shown up as we scanned the crowd looking for familiar faces. Most were still dressed in their special Easter clothes. Seeing so many people I wondered, for the first time, if I would be able to find the golden egg. Dave was nervous too because I had told him that when I won the red Schwinn racer, he could have the Beast, which was certainly better than having no bike at all.

"How did everyone find out about the egg hunt Dave?" I asked.

"I don't know, I didn't tell anyone, did you?" asked Dave.

"Heck no, I don't even see anybody I know. Who are all these people anyway? What am I going to do now? How am I going to find the golden egg with all these kids looking too?"

We cruised over to the park's pavilion on the Beast and parked it by the bike rack. I didn't bother to lock it up because nobody wanted to steal an old girl's bike. We wandered around looking for anybody that we knew. My stomach was doing flip-flops. I started feeling queasy, when I saw all of the kids that had come to the egg hunt. I'd never seen so many kids in one place.

Quickly, I realized that I needed a better strategy than just being the fastest. Most of the kids had brought their straw Easter baskets so that they could pick up lots of the eggs and candy lying in the grass. I hadn't brought my Easter basket because I only wanted to find the golden egg and win the bike. I had plenty of candy, and I didn't want to be slowed down carrying an Easter basket.

The only person I saw that I knew was B.O. Bodeen. His dad was president of the Knights of Columbus men's club. B.O.'s real name was Ralph and he was a couple of years older than me. I didn't like him or any of the Bodeens, but I decided that going up to him was my best shot at getting some help. I should have known better.

The Bodeens lived on our street, and they were known for many things—none of them good. Nobody understood how Mr. Bodeen, a hard-looking man, had gotten to be the president of the Knights of Columbus, but he did. Some of the members had even threatened to quit, but to no avail. He was still the K of C president. The best news that I had heard was that the Bodeens were going to move out of our neighborhood this summer.

Nothing stirred up our neighborhood like a family moving out and a new family moving to the neighborhood. If a person was lucky enough to meet the new neighbors before everybody else, he or she was a celebrity and everybody visited to find out any secrets.

A neighbor moving away was an especially anxious time for the neighbors living on either side of the new neighbor. Depending on who was moving out and who was moving in, it might have been better for the old neighbors to stay even if they were bad neighbors. But in this case, no one wanted the Bodeens to stay, no matter who was moving into their house.

The Bodeens had kids our ages, and they always smelled bad. That is why we nicknamed Ralph "B.O." for 'body odor.' Ralph was the oldest Bodeen kid, and he was always trying to build and launch a rocket ship that he made out of the free matches from the Rexall drugstore. The Bodeen daughter was just as strange. But, if the kids were weird, the parents were freaky.

Mr. Bodeen was always loud and Mrs. Bodeen dyed her long, ratted hair jet black. She looked like a real-life witch. She even had hairy moles on her chin and nose. And what was even weirder was that on Halloween, she dressed like a witch to give out candy to the kids that were brave enough to knock on her door. Now tell me, who would dress like a real witch, if she looked like a real witch, unless she was a real witch?

I would go trick or treating to the Bodeen's house just to peek inside, but I would never eat their candy. Joey said their candy was made from all the cats and dogs that had been lost in our neighborhood. Nobody knew for sure where the Bodeens were moving, and nobody really cared, but our parents would always smile and say hello to them.

I tried to warm B.O. up by acting like I was interested in him and his family before I asked him about the egg hunt. B.O. wasn't very good looking and I felt somewhat sorry looking at him. He was tall and skinny and although he was only 14 years old, he needed a shave really bad. His black plastic eyeglass frames were broken in two places, and they were held together with dirty white adhesive tape. B.O. smelled so bad, you didn't want to get too close even on Easter Sunday.

I acted nonchalant and interested, "Where are you moving B.O., I mean Ralph?"

"Why should I tell you pip-squeak? Do you think you're my girlfriend? I don't want you calling me sweetheart you little sissy," he said in his nasally irritating voice.

Well in that one instant, I was reminded why nobody liked him and I wanted to pop him right in his jaw, but instead I said, "Yeah, well I thought, I'd ask you just to be friendly that's all Ralph."

"Well, don't be nice you little punk, what do you want anyway?"

"I was just going to ask you about the egg hunt that's all."

"Do you think you're going win that bike baby face? You're not. You'll never find that golden egg," smirked B.O. and with that he turned his back and walked away laughing.

I was so angry and felt so mad at B.O. that I started spitting, when I tried to speak. My words came out blubbering. Luckily, Dave grabbed my arm and said, "Come on Mickey. We don' need that jerk's help. Let's go ask somebody else."

As I stalked away fuming, B.O. looked back over his shoulder and smirked, "Oh the little babies got their feelings hurt, and now their running away. Sorry little girlies. I didn't mean to hurt your feelings," and then he laughed this really loud, nasally nasty laugh.

As I walked away, my face got redder as I got madder because he was mocking me. I wondered how he knew that I wanted to win that bike.

Without B.O.'s help, we walked around trying to figure out how to find the right egg hunt. Each hunt was designed for different ages of kids.

Catholics take their earthly lives very seriously because their trip to heaven depends on it. They always try their best. In other words, there's a lot riding on how you live your life. Easter egg hunts are no exception. Everybody I saw that day was taking this egg hunt very seriously.

Fathers and mothers were practicing with their kids to pick up eggs and put them into their baskets. Some of the fathers even got a little upset with their kids if they didn't take the practice seriously enough. Mothers were usually laughing, but not the dads. The egg hunt was serious business for them and for me.

As we walked and gawked at everyone, I heard a loud voice that sounded like a man talking into an aluminum trashcan. He was walking through the crowd with a megaphone the size of a kitchen garbage can and I heard him scream, "The First Annual Knights of Columbus Easter Egg Hunt will begin in five minutes. Everyone should go to their respective areas right now!"

I panicked as I looked at Dave and put my palms up in the air and stammered, "Where are we supposed to go?"

"I don't know Mickey," he answered.

And with that, I started trotting in circles. My trot turned into a full speed gallop, when I realized there was a series of large areas marked off with orange tape. Kids were getting into groups with kids their own age. The further into the park I ran, the older the kids were.

Finally, I saw a man wearing an apron that said, "Knight of Columbus" in thick red letters across his chest. I yelled to him without stopping, "Where is the egg hunt for the red Schwinn racer?"

"At the very end of the park," he yelled back, "but you look too young for that hunt, why don't you stay here kid?"

"No thanks," I yelled back over my shoulder, "I want to win that racer. Come on Dave," and we took off like rockets looking for the older guys' Easter egg hunt.

Dave was trying to keep up with me, but I was a lot faster so he chased me the whole way there. We had been playing with Joey's older friends since we were little kids. Dave was the only friend I had my own age, so I was not surprised, when I got to the last egg hunt and saw a bunch of Joey's friends waiting for the red Schwinn racer hunt to begin.

When he saw me running towards him, Mike said, "How is it going Mickey? Where's Joey? What're you doing here? You should be with kids your own age."

"I'm going to win that big red racer not a bag of candy Mike," I said as I trotted along and evaluated the other guys standing along the orange tape. I was waiting for Dave, while I was looking for the best spot to start the egg hunt. My mind was working as fast as my feet, when out of the corner of my eye I saw B.O. sitting off to the side by himself looking cunningly across the field through his broken black plastic glasses.

As I surveyed the grassy area, there were a couple of locations that looked promising, but seeing B.O. sitting by himself looked pretty suspicious to me, even though nobody wanted to sit next to him because he stunk so bad.

B.O. looked as guilty as sin. That is when the best idea I ever had hit me right between the eyes. I ran over to B.O. and said more than asked, "Looks like a good spot to me, you don't mind if I start here do you B.O.?" I emphasized his nasty nickname.

"Get out of here, you little dip wad," growled B.O. as he sat there in the grass trying to not look guilty.

"No, I am going to stay right here with you, B.O. because you are my girlfriend," I said mocking him.

"Get out of here, you little punk" he ordered as he took a swipe at me with his dirty paw.

Ducking, I said," You can't make me B.O. It's a free country ain't it? I can stand wherever I want," then I braced myself in case he did hit me. Looking the area over I didn't see the golden egg anywhere obvious and the level of my excitement was higher than during a fire drill at school. I felt sure B.O. was going to cheat.

The *"Crrraaacck!"* of the starting gun suddenly split the air and the egg hunt was immediately afoot as all of the kids' eyes hit the ground along with their feet. Everybody was searching for the golden egg.

Instinctively, I blasted past the orange tape and B.O., but looking back over my shoulder, I realized the mistake of letting B.O. out of my sight. I decided to stay just a couple of yards in front of him so that I could watch him and scan the area in front of me at the same time. I planned to spot the egg just a moment before him and then I was going to sprint to the golden egg and grab it.

I wanted to be close, but not so close that B.O. could grab me. I watched his squinty, guilty eyes closely so that he would tip me off as to where the golden egg was hidden. The more his reptile-like eyes snaked back and forth across the field, the more I was sure that he was cheating, but I didn't have any idea where the golden egg was. For a moment, I wondered if I was cheating too by following B.O., the cheater.

We jogged to the middle of the field playing cat and mouse. Still I didn't see the golden egg, but nobody else had found it either and you could tell B.O. was getting real nervous. Everybody was dashing around madly in search of the golden egg.

I was dying to see the bright sun reflect off of the golden egg before anybody else. I had been dreaming about that red Schwinn racer, and all of the places I was going to ride it for weeks. My chest was pounding and my stomach was churning as B.O. led me around the park dodging trees looking for the golden egg.

All of the sudden B.O. turned about face in mid-stride and raced back towards the area where we had started the hunt. I quickly saw that he was racing towards a small pine tree near the starting line. I blasted off like a jet fighter plane to chase him down and run him into the ground. I knew I was going to pass him and get to the golden egg first.

I was running as fast and hard as I could. My legs and arms were pumping and my feet verily flew over the ground as I bolted after B.O. towards the tree. My lungs felt like they would explode, I was breathing so hard and fast.

B.O. was shocked, when I raced past him. The tree was only about 25 yards away, when I saw the sun glint off something shiny at the foot of the little tree. My legs and feet leaped into yet a higher gear. I was zooming so fast now that my feet barely touched the ground. I thought I was actually flying!

Exhilaration filled my soul at the thought of finding the golden egg and the red Schwinn racer as I blasted across the last ten yards. As I flew, I searched for the glint of the golden egg once again so that I could pinpoint the target of my headlong dive to the bottom of the tree mulch.

As my radar-sense frantically searched the base of the tree, I saw a hand reaching around the trunk of the small pine tree. The hand was searching for something. I couldn't see the face of the person who owned the hand, but it sure looked like the hand was reaching for the golden egg. With all of the strength and energy I could muster, I dove headfirst toward the tree. It was the fastest way to pluck the golden egg from its nest.

As I soared through the air, the hand under the tree snatched the golden egg, and I crash-landed headfirst into the tree's black, stinky, steamy mulch. My heart was broken. My eyes stung as I lay there in disbelief on the verge of crying. On the other side of the tree, someone hollered hysterically, "I got it, I got it. Mickey I got the golden egg!"

Who is that, I wondered? Was that Dave yelling? Then I realized it was Dave yelling. I couldn't believe it. I was so close to grabbing the golden egg, but Dave found it instead.

He came running around the tree jumping ecstatically up and down and squealing that he had found the golden egg. At first, when Dave saw me lying on my back in the mulch he asked, "Mickey, why are you laying in the dirt?' Then in mid-sentence he realized what must've happened. He had found the golden egg a split second before me.

"Here Mickey," he said as he held out the golden egg to me, "You take it. You tried a lot harder than me. I was just standing there waiting for you to find it, when I thought I'd look under the tree. That's all I did. You take the egg Mickey," as he continued to hold the golden egg out to me.

Well in that one frozen moment in time, a million thoughts whirled through my mind, while my broken heart and spirit tried to make sense of everything that had just happened. I would be lying if I said that I wasn't sorely tempted to snatch the golden egg from Dave's hand.

Dave was right. I had tried harder. Heck, Dave didn't even really care about the Easter egg hunt. I talked him into coming with me because I wanted to win "The Rocket," and I didn't want to go alone. Nobody would blame me for taking the golden egg that Dave offered to me. I had already promised to give him the Black Beast, when I won, so we would both have bikes.

Although my thoughts seemed fair, they just didn't feel right in my head and in my heart. The fact was Dave found the golden egg and nothing could change that one simple fact. He had won, fair and square. He didn't cheat like B.O. was trying to do. Dave found the golden egg first—fairly.

"No," I said, sure of my answer, "It's yours Dave, you won fair and square. Now we both have bikes to ride. You keep the golden egg Dave. The Rocket is yours."

As Dave put the egg in his pocket, he grew the biggest smile on his face I had ever seen him have. We raced to the park pavilion where Dave exchanged the golden egg for the Rocket. *The Star* newspaper was there to take Dave's picture holding his red Schwinn racer by its handlebars.

Dave wanted me in the photograph too because I was his best friend. I did, but it hurt pretty bad seeing Dave hold the Rocket and knowing that I wasn't going to ride The Rocket home.

Afterwards, we rode down the street side-by-side, Dave on the Rocket and me on the Black Beast, but things didn't feel quite right. I was getting used to the fact that I didn't win and that Dave did, so that wasn't it. We were best friends. It was something else.

All of the sudden, it dawned on me. I missed Dave's hands holding on to my shoulders helping me keep my balance as I pedaled.

As I jumped up on the big, leather cushy seat to coast alongside of Dave, I felt the bright sunshine and the cool spring air on my face. I felt great!

As we coasted along, I looked down at the mulch stains on my sweatshirt and the newly torn hole in the knee of my blue jeans. I was sure glad I had changed out of my Easter clothes or there would have been some real trouble at home. I chuckled at the thought. Yeah, things were going to be different now that Dave and I each had our own bike.

"Let's play follow-the-leader, Dave!" I yelled over my shoulder as I jumped down to my pedals and raced ahead of him on the Beast to be the leader.

"Okay, but I get to be the leader next!"

Chapter 3

Big Fish Story

ridays aren't my favorite day of the week although they should be. During school, Friday is the beginning of the weekend and the end of a hard week, but Fridays don't even matter during the summer. Its one redeeming grace is that I don't have to go to bed at my regular bedtime because I don't have to go to school or go to church the next day.

Everyone looks forward to Friday, but not me. As a Catholic, I can't eat meat on Fridays and in my house that only leaves a couple of other menu options. We either have Kroger's frozen fish sticks, tuna salad, egg salad, tuna casserole or on a rare occasion scrambled eggs and toast. We also have salads or canned vegetables and fruit with most of our dinners.

Since Catholics can't eat meat on Fridays, there are only two good things about eating on Friday. The first is that Mom will, on a rare occasion, give me a jelly sandwich for lunch. The second reason is the St. Kevin's Mother's Club Fish Fry Dinner that's held on the first Friday of every month in the school cafeteria during the school year.

The Fish Fry dinner food doesn't really taste very good, but afterwards the kids hang out with their friends on the school playground, while the parents visit with their friends. Imagine, it's like going to a restaurant with a playground. The seventh and eighth grade girls and boys take turns serving the food and cleaning up after everybody as their community service.

It isn't that my family's meals are all that special the other days of the week. It's just that Fridays aren't special at all. Dad gives Mom $30 dollars a week to run the household, which includes everything. That is not much money for Mom to buy gourmet food. The only steaks we eat are bought in Kroger's frozen food section. They're called Salisbury steaks, and the square pieces of ground meat are swimming in an aluminum pan full of gelatin-like brown gravy. The steaks are so small that I have to eat at least two pieces of buttered white bread with the extra gravy ladled on them to fill me up. It seems like the older I get the more white bread I eat.

We don't live in grand opulence in my neighborhood. We live in the age of modern suburban efficiency and convenience. We complain about having to load and empty the electric dishwasher. Every type of food that once was lovingly made by a mother's hands is now prepackaged and frozen in plastic, aluminum foil, or canned at some factory and stored in our cupboard.

Anybody in our family can make dinner as long as he or she can open a can and dump it into a saucepan or take the frozen package out of the freezer and stick it in the oven at 350 degrees for an hour. My favorite treat is to eat a whole can of greasy red tamales that are wrapped in paper, when I am at home because I stayed home from school—sick. Modern appliances are meant to give modern mothers time to do other modern day chores, like vacuuming the wall-to-wall carpet or defrosting the "ice box," while they cook dinner in their modern, slick, efficient, and chromed kitchen.

It was the evening of the May Fish Fry that I learned the real value of having an older brother like Joey. Joey was a charmer with a million-dollar smile.

The girls and their mothers really liked Joey. He was always grinning and telling the girls something to make them giggle and laugh. They thought he was the funniest guy in the world. They laughed at everything he said— even if it wasn't very funny.

At this Fish Fry, Joey had a couple of the girls in his class laughing and screeching out on the playground, which created quite an opportunity for me. Two girls in Joey's class didn't like each other, but they each 'liked' Joey. The prettiest and shyest one thought the best route to Joey's heart was through me. Her name was Tina.

Tina was beautiful; she even looked pretty in her plaid school uniform with white knee socks. The other girl's name was Pauline. Mom had warned Joey about Pauline, saying she was too bold and always pushy. I thought Pauline was 'phony.' I liked Tina best and so did Joey, but wherever Joey went Pauline was sure to follow.

After I ate my breaded and baked fish stick dinner that was served on an aluminum school tray with macaroni and cheese, canned green beans and a buttered roll, I went outside to play soccer with my school buddies. When I chased the soccer ball downfield, I noticed Tina standing over by the school building waving at me and calling my name. Well, it took me about a half of a second to decide to run over and see what she wanted. Tina was so pretty and sweet, I was happy to have her attention and just stand by her.

As I looked up into her big, beautiful hazel eyes with golden flecks, I instantly became hypnotized by her innocence and natural beauty. Instantly, I became jealous for her attention and I didn't want to share her with anyone. Feeling roguish, I slowly strolled around the corner of the building, where nobody could see us, and she shyly followed me.

Tina confided in me that she really liked Joey a lot, but wondered if he liked Pauline better than her. She asked me what she should do to get more of Joey's attention.

"Have you ever told Joey how much you like him?" I asked adoringly, wishing that she liked me more than Joey.

"Are you kidding?" asked Tina, "I'd die first, it's too embarrassing." "Well how is he supposed to know you like him then? You have to tell him. Pauline follows Joey around like she is his mom," I said feeling like Ann Landers, the personal advice columnist, in the *St. Louis Post-Dispatch*.

"I know; Pauline never gives me a chance to talk to Joey at school alone. Would you ask him who he likes best Mickey—*please*?" she pleaded.

Well, I thought I'd die right there standing in the long shadow of the classroom building. The longer Tina looked at me the harder and faster my heart pounded. At that precise moment, I decided that Joey wasn't good enough for Tina. She was too innocent and perfect for him. It would be better for her if she fell in love with me, and I felt larceny in my heart. I intended for us to live happily ever after.

"Well," I proclaimed, "Joey ain't good enough for you. You should be my girlfriend Tina."

Well the way she laughed, when I said that, you would've thought I was Johnny Carson doing a monologue on his *Tonight Show*. She didn't realize that I was dead serious, so I played along like I was just kidding around although my heart was broken.

"Oh, you're just like Joey, you're both so funny, but I don't think he'll ever like me," she tittered. Well I knew right then and there that Tina and I would never be girlfriend and boyfriend no matter how much I loved her so I decided on a different gambit.

"Aww shoot Tina, Joey likes you plenty. All you have to do is give him a big hug and a kiss, that's all. That's what Joey told me Pauline did," I lied in my most charming manner.

Putting her hands on her hips, she innocently asked, "Are you sure Pauline kissed Joey Mickey?"

Pangs of guilt shook me and I knew that if I lied anymore, I would end up in the confessional with Father Christiansen, but I couldn't stop myself from lying and smiling. I was smitten.

"Well that's what Joey told me. I'll bet you're a great kisser," I said trying to look as charming as Joey.

"Actually, I've never kissed anyone besides people in my family," she confided in me as I blushed with the knowledge of my guilty thoughts.

"Never?" I asked incredulously, and then I said reassuringly, "Well all you have to do is practice a little and you'll be fine."

"Well who's going to practice with me?" she asked as my lies came to me easily.

"Well, the girls tell me I am a pretty good kisser," I claimed, which actually wasn't a lie. Both Mom and Grandma told me I was a good kisser and a good hugger. Although I had never kissed a girl my age, I would have lied to my own Mom to kiss Tina smack on the lips.

"Well I don't know. I'd feel funny if I kissed you. You're so young," she cooed.

"All we have to do is kiss once. Then, I'll tell you if you're a good kisser so you won't be afraid to kiss Joey." I was telling lies so smoothly and with such sincerity even I believed them.

The thought of kissing Tina drove me wild with desire. If I admitted my lies to Father Christiansen, he would've had me saying penance prayers for hours.

"Well I don't know," she said more as a question than a statement.

Feeling confident and emboldened by my lies, I jumped onto a short red brick retaining wall so I was as tall as Tina and grabbed her into my arms in an awkward hug. She didn't resist, but I sensed that she felt more awkward than rapturous. Quickly, I smooched my lips to hers and kind of moved my face around and moaned for what seemed like an eternity. I didn't know whether to stop smooching and yell a victory chant or just keep canoodling. I opted for the latter.

Tina was the prettiest girl at St. Kevin and the simple thought of her made me muzzy-headed. She enjoyed kissing me too. She never budged. We stood clinging to each other as our embrace softened in the golden glow of twilight as the sun dipped below the playground.

My guilt and the sensations that coursed through my body were impossible to distinguish. I was a rogue and an adoring bon vivant at the same time. I didn't feel like I was ten years old. I felt like a grown man holding the woman that I would love and cherish forever.

Lost in our moment, we were startled, when Sister Peter yelled at us from the nun's Convent patio, "Who's there? What's going on over there? You'd better not be doing what I think you're doing."

"Quick, run, before she catches us," I whispered to Tina as I gazed into her sparkling golden hazel eyes one last time. And with that, we dashed around the school building still holding hands, neither of us feeling awkward or embarrassed about our secret.

"You're sure a great kisser," I crowed fishing for a compliment in return.

"I sure hope Joey thinks so," she giggled as we each ran our separate ways. Although I never kissed Tina again, I never forgot she was my first kiss, and I prayed she didn't forget I was hers. I never told anybody, especially not Father Christiansen or Joey.

Chapter 4

Over the St. Charles Rock Road, And Through Forest Park To the City and Grandma's House I Go!

As I walked home after school, I was trying to think of something to do because it was a nothing-special egg salad sandwich Friday. That's when I saw Grandma's car parked in front of our house. I broke into a mad dash and stormed through the front door yelling her name loudly, "Hey Grandma!"

Grandma's visits are always special. They always mean something fun is going to happen and it's impossible not to recognize her car. She drives a gray

1959 Plymouth Plaza with huge red tail light fins. We call her car the 'Ol' Gray Mare,' because Grandma drives sooooo slooooowly you wonder if she is asleep at the wheel. The Ol' Gray Mare has a three-speed manual transmission on the column, but it doesn't matter because Grandma only uses first and second gears, when she drives.

Everybody always kids Grandma that she could've saved a fortune, when she bought the Ol' Gray Mare, if she hadn't paid for that third gear, but she just ignores everybody, when we kid her. It was true though; Grandma always drove on every street in second gear. She never used third gear—ever. As she drives merrily along, people honk their horns incessantly trying to get her to drive faster, but she'd never drives fast enough to shift into third gear. She doesn't care one iota what anybody says or does; she drives the speed that makes her feel safe.

She would always declare in a disgustedly superior way, "Oh what's wrong with them? They don't need to drive any faster than we're going right now. What's their hurry? Are they going to a fire?" When she would hear men yell and scream at her and wave their fists, she would just look straight ahead and hand crank up her car window even if it was a hot summer day. We didn't know anyone that had air conditioning in his or her car. Grandma wouldn't even give the person the satisfaction of even glancing in their direction. When their behavior became overly loud or obscene, she would quietly mutter, "Commoner," like it was the biggest insult in the world because from Grandma, it was. "Acting common" was the one behavior Grandma didn't tolerate from anybody—especially us.

Grandma is my best friend. It's my dream that one day she will come to live with us, but deep in my heart, I know she never will. She loves living in her own home. She had lived with her mother, my great-grandmother, who we called Gigi, until Gigi died a few years ago. Ever since then, Grandma lived alone. My Grandpa was a medical doctor, but he died before I was born. Grandma never even dated after Grandpa died. She always said that she could never love anyone other than him. That is the way Grandma is—definite.

She never raised her voice or spanked me. She didn't have to; I always did what she wanted because I never wanted to disappoint her—ever.

I found Grandma as quickly as I could and gave her the biggest and strongest hug she had ever had. Then I said, "Good God-Grandma, you're here!" That was our private joke. Grandma was my baptismal Godmother. I called her my "Good, God-Grandma" and she loved it.

Acting like I had squeezed the breath out of her, she put her hands on my shoulders, gave me a hug and a kiss on both of my cheeks and said, "How's my Mickey today?" Grandma smelled like Ivory soap and sugar, I loved it.

"Great, now that you're here Grandma. Are you going to stay for dinner and play some games tonight? Checkers? Why don't you spend the whole weekend Grandma?" I rattled off breathlessly.

"Whoa cowboy! You're going way too fast for me. No. I'm sorry I can't stay with your family this weekend. I've got a special friend coming to stay with me at my house," she said with a smile.

Well, to say I was broken-hearted is an understatement. I was crushed. I could accept that Grandma had other plans and couldn't stay long, but who was the special friend she mentioned? I was Grandma's special friend, maybe Joey, but definitely me.

"Who's your special friend Grandma?" I asked nervously, afraid of her answer.

"You, you goofy cowboy," she said as she patted me on my head and looked me in the eye, "Do you want to spend the weekend at my house? I promise we'll have a lot of fun if you do. Please Mickey?" she pleaded.

I had been so sad that it took a moment for me to understand what Grandma had said. She was inviting me to spend the weekend with her at her house. Spending the weekend at Grandma's was very special because she would do anything that I wanted to do. I was so excited and happy it felt like I was bursting. Then I decided I would trick her back.

Mock seriously I said, "I don't know Grandma. I have a lot of stuff to do this weekend. I'm not sure I can, because I'm pretty busy. I have to take out the garbage and clean my room and lots of other stuff too."

After telling her all those things, she acted really sad so I immediately told her, "I'm just kidding Grandma, I'll come with you," and with that she perked up and I ran to my room to pack my stuff.

That is when I remembered that I hadn't even asked Mom. In fact, I hadn't even said hello to Mom because I was so happy to see my Grandma. Trying to look apologetic, I walked into the kitchen again, "Hi Mom," I said with a big smile, "May I go to Grandma's?" as I walked over and gave her a big hug.

"Sure Mickey and you don't have to worry about packing your stuff, I already have your suitcase packed."

"Wow! Thanks Mom, you're the best! I'm ready whenever you are Grandma," and with that we said our goodbyes and headed out for our big city adventure in the Ol' Gray Mare.

Each of us kids got our own special weekends with Grandma, and believe me, it was special from beginning to end. "What are we going to do first Grandma? I asked as we moseyed towards her house on Potomac Street in south St. Louis with the cars honking behind us.

"Well first I thought we'd stop at the new W.T. Grant's store next to St. Ann Bank so you can pick out a plastic model that you can build over the weekend at my house. What do you think of that idea Mickey?"

"Neat-O Grandma," I said, as she parked the Ol' Gray Mare in Grant's brand new, smooth-as-glass, black asphalt parking lot that was bigger than Pattonville High School's football field. It had huge parking lot lights that were taller than any building in St. Ann and they made it look like daylight all of the time.

W.T. Grant's had everything a modern family could use. Clothes, cosmetics, home supplies and small pets like parakeets and gold fish. Best of all, Grant's had lots of comic books, toys and games. In the toy department, Grant's had the largest and best selection of Revell, AMT, and Hawk's plastic models that I had ever seen. It had two entire aisles, both sides, dedicated to plastic models, glue, paint and other model supplies. Grandma knew I liked to visit Grant's because it had models of cars, trucks, airplanes, ships and even movie monsters like Frankenstein, the Wolfman and Dracula. Many models cost a buck or two, but large navy ships like aircraft carriers were a lot more expensive and a lot harder to put together. She liked the Grant's store because it had a housewares department.

I had been building models for the past couple of years and I had a pretty good collection that I displayed on the shelves in my bedroom. I would get plastic models as gifts or buy them with the money I had earned by cutting grass, collecting bottles for their two-cent deposit, and shoveling snow in the winter. We saved every penny we earned to buy the things our parents wouldn't buy like candy bars, ice cream cones and games of pinball.

As I closely inspected the model airplanes, Grandma went searching for a new modern can-opener. Grant's had bi-wing airplanes, jets and bombers from the First and Second World Wars, some new modern jets and even a helicopter. I thought I knew a lot about airplanes because we lived so near St. Louis' Lambert Airport, and my uncle had been an airplane pilot in the war.

I liked jet airplanes, but they were loud. Most days, you could hear McDonnell-Douglass jets and Lambert's airliners flying right over our heads. Some days, I even heard loud explosions in the sky that couldn't be seen as the jets flew overhead and broke the sound barrier. The explosions were so loud they'd rattle the glass in our windows and rattle the china and keepsakes in the cabinets in our homes.

The guys and I had just hiked over to and explored Lambert Airport a couple of weeks ago. It was the first time we had snuck over there. It was really cool and there was hardly a soul there on the Sunday afternoon that we went to explore. We had the whole terminal to ourselves. Always in search of some quick cash to buy stuff, we quickly discovered that the airport travelers left nickels, dimes and quarters in the rows upon rows of black Ma Bell pay telephones. So we spent the first part of the afternoon checking the coin returns of hundreds of pay phones on both floors of the main copper-topped terminal. It seemed like almost every phone had at least a nickel or dime in it. It was a gold mine of loose coins!

With the loose change we found, we each bought a hamburger and soda. Afterwards, we played every pinball game in the terminal the rest of the afternoon. It was a great way to spend a Sunday, and we planned to go back. Of course, we didn't tell our parents or our other friends either.

In my model airplane collection, I already had a Mustang P-51, a P-38 Lightning, which had a cool wing design, and a World War I Sopwith Camel biplane. Joey had a Messerschmitt.

After carefully assessing the different styles of model airplanes, I decided to buy a car. I couldn't decide between a cool 1934 Ford Coupe, which could be built stock or customized into a hot rod with flame decals, and a stock 1957 T-Bird.

I liked the Ford Thunderbird hardtop convertible because my next-door-neighbor, Chuck McKinley, drove a white T-Bird just like it with a red interior. Chuck was a world-famous tennis player. He had won the U.S. National Championships Men's Singles last summer. Jack Buck, one of the Cardinals' announcers said, "Chuck is so good, they've already named the McKinley Bridge and McKinley High School after him!" Chuck was a real celebrity in our neighborhood, especially when the TV stations came to his house after big wins. We loved Chuck, but none of us could play tennis very well because we didn't have any tennis courts in St. Ann.

I decided on the hot rod version of the 1934 coupe, and Grandma found a new can-opener so off we went—cruising down the St. Charles Rock Road in the Ol' Gray Mare toward the city. After we arrived at Grandma's house on Potomac Street, I ran over to the Kennard Elementary School's huge playground, and played with some new friends named Joe and Mike that I met while Grandma fixed dinner.

Waking up at Grandma's was always special. Her home was always quieter and neater than ours, and when I walked into her kitchen, she would be there smiling in her robe asking me what I wanted for breakfast. She had already read the morning edition of the *St. Louis Globe-Democrat* newspaper that had been delivered by a driver in a black carriage pulled by a large white horse with a black leather harness. The same driver, horse and carriage would come back in the afternoon to deliver the

St. Louis Post-Dispatch, but Grandma only read the morning paper.

While Grandma fixed us each a bowl of Kellogg's Corn Flakes cereal with a sliced up banana and a glass of orange juice, I asked her what she wanted to do.

"I have a grand adventure planned for us Mickey as soon as we eat breakfast and get dressed."

"What're we going to do Grandma?"

"I can't tell you until you're dressed, and ready to leave. It's a secret I've been planning."

Well, nothing gets kid moving faster than the idea that a secret is about to be discovered. Lickety-split, we were marching down the alley behind her house, cutting over to one street and then down another. The whole time we walked, I pestered her with questions about our adventure, but she wouldn't give it away. All of the sudden she stopped at a street corner and announced triumphantly, "We're here Mickey." As I looked around quizzically, I realized that we were standing at a bus stop on Oleatha Avenue.

"Are we going take a bus, Grandma?"

"You bet we are."

"Where are we going?" I asked apprehensively because I had never been on a bus.

"Downtown."

"In the city Grandma? Are we going to see Santa Claus?"

"How could we see Santa, Mickey? He's at the North Pole with Mrs. Claus and his elves at this time of year."

"Well what are we going to do in Downtown then?" I was confused. We only drove downtown two times a year. One, to buy our Easter clothes at either Stix, Baer & Fuller, Famous-Barr or Boyd's, and two, to sit on Santa's lap to tell him what we wanted for Christmas and see all of the decorated Christmas windows at the department stores. My favorites were the huge corner windows that had lots of different electric trains whizzing in and out of tunnels with lots of toys stuffed around the tracks.

"We're going to have all kinds of adventures Mickey, all kinds," she said confidently, as she smiled, and looked out straight ahead with her black leather purse draped over her left arm and her hands clasped at her waist. Oh, how I loved my Grandma!

Grandma was brave. She had left her childhood home and family in Vincennes, Indiana and come to St. Louis to study nursing, when she was just 19 years old. She came in 1915, and she didn't know anybody in St. Louis. She met my grandfather, when she was in nursing school, and Grandfather was at St. Louis University's medical school studying to be a doctor. He had come from Brunswick, Missouri by way of Sedalia. I had never met my Grandfather. He died before I was born, when Mom was just five-years old. I was always sad that I didn't know him.

Grandma was very practical. Everything she said, ate, did, or wore was practical. Every day she wore one of a dozen or so colorful prints, but simple jersey knit or cotton dresses that she carefully hung in her closet after they were washed, hung to dry and ironed. If it was cool, she wore one of her several wool or cotton sweaters, and if it was real cold she wore her winter coat and gloves. I never saw her wear pants, shorts or a swimsuit. She always wore a pair of her practical and simple black leather slip-on shoes that were great for walking because they had very low rubber heels. As a nurse, she was always walking and she was proud of her shapely legs. She always carried her purse over her left arm. It held her keys, tissues and billfold, which always had the exact change for anything that she bought. She paid cash for everything.

I had never taken a bus trip anywhere, much less downtown, and the thought of it gave me the heebie-jeebies.

"Why don't we just drive the Ol' Gray Mare Grandma?"

"Well that wouldn't be an adventure, would it? Come on Mickey, this will be fun, I promise. Have you ever taken a bus before?"

"No," I said feeling pretty unsure of our situation. "Have you?"

"Have I? Let me tell you this Mickey, your Grandfather Herbert drove a trolley all over St. Louis to put himself through medical school, and I proudly sat right next to him on my days off. We must've driven down every street in St. Louis together," she laughed looking longingly up into the brilliant blue sky with a beautiful smile on her face. You could tell she still loved Grandfather.

"This is an adventure, and you're going to do something completely different than you've ever done before," and with that the bus pulled up and stopped at the curb with its brakes screeching. We stepped on the bus. Grandma pulled out the exact change for our fares and transfers and we walked to about the middle of the bus before we found an empty seat to share.

"Why don't you sit next to the window Mickey, so you can see well," she commanded more than asked.

As I cautiously slid over to the window, I looked at all of the people sitting on the bus. Most did not pay any attention to us, and seemed to be lost in their own affairs staring silently ahead or absently out of the window, a few were asleep. No one was talking to one and other. One man was muttering to himself and had an earplug stuck into his ear. He was listening to a small transistor radio that was in his front shirt pocket. I smiled because I planned to ask for a Magnavox transistor radio for my birthday, so I could listen to Cardinals' games in my bed at night, and everyone would think I was asleep. Clever me.

Suddenly, a couple of wet, little hands covered my eyes. Startled, I pulled the hands from my eyes. As I turned around, I was staring into a pair of intent, blue eyes, and what looked like a little girl sticking her tongue out at me.

"Bet, you can't tickle me?" she said.

Annoyed I said, "You're right. I bet I can't either," and turned back around to mind my own business. Now, I knew why people stared off into space at nothing on the bus. They didn't want to get stuck talking with someone that didn't interest them.

As the bus lumbered down the street, I looked out the opened window and watched grown-ups and kids as they walked along on the sidewalks across the street and watched the cars as they zoomed by the bus—everyone looked like they were in a rush.

"What are you looking at Mickey?"

"Those people. Where are they going Grandma?"

"Well that one is going to the bakery for some coffee cake," she declared pointing to a woman pulling a small wire basket on wheels.

"Really? Wow how do you know that?" I asked.

Grandma laughed, "She's my neighbor, Mrs. Rosenmeier. She walks to her favorite bakery every Saturday morning. Some Saturdays she brings me a piece of cake after she gets home, and I make a cup of tea for the both of us, that's how."

"Wow you're good. What about him? Do you know him too?"

"He's walking down to the park's baseball fields to watch the kids play."

"Is he your neighbor too Grandma?"

"No. I'm just making up a story about him. I don't really know who he is," she snickered. "I make up stories about people I see all of the time. It's a fun way to pass the time. Do you want to try?"

"That's a good idea Grandma. I'll play. See that little girl? She's running away from her older sister who is really mean, and I'll bet that little boy is riding his brother's bike real fast because he doesn't want to get caught taking it."

"Those are great stories Mickey. Now it's my turn. See that woman with the books in her arms? She's a teacher and she's rushing to the library to return some overdue books."

After swapping other people's made-up stories for what seemed like a long time, Grandma pulled a cord that was draped over my head that I hadn't noticed. It rang a bell that told the bus driver someone needed to get off of the bus. "We're getting off at the next stop, so stay close to me Mickey," she announced.

I was darn disappointed that our bus ride was over already. I enjoyed people watching. "Okay Grandma," I said as I followed her down the aisle. We thanked the bus driver as we stepped off the bus onto the curb of the street.

"Holy cow, we're downtown Grandma and that's the whatchamacallit store, where I see Santa every year. Too bad he's at the North Pole. I'll bet there's no line to see him today." Grandma just smiled as she led us into the Famous-Barr department store.

"What are we looking for Grandma?"

"First, we're going to the stamp and coin collection department. I want to ask someone about my collections."

Grandma had two collections she prized, her stamps and her coins. They weren't big fancy collections kept in a big, steel safe with a lock. She kept them in an assortment of small, white boxes that she kept in her dresser drawer. She really enjoyed showing them to the grandkids and telling us how she found each coin.

I followed Grandma up the escalator for several floors until we found the coin and stamp department. There was no one in the department, except for a man nattily dressed in a dark suit, white shirt and dark tie. He seemed tall, and my hackles went up because I distrusted him immediately. His dark hair was combed back into a greasy pompadour and his mustache was neatly trimmed. He had an oily look. His big toothy smile seemed phony.

The man greeted us with a booming voice that was dripping with sugar and southern sarcasm, "Good morning Madame may I help you?"

Through the sound of his voice and his dress and mannerisms, he seemed like a snake oil salesman to me, but I couldn't tell if Grandma trusted him or not because she smiled at everyone.

"Well thank you sir," she said, "Yes you may. I was wondering if you be kind enough to give me an idea of the value of my collections?"

Tapping his fingertips together in front of his chest he replied, "I would be happy to assist you Madame. May I inspect them please?" as he grandly waved us over to a glass display case that had a black velvet mat spread across the top of it.

Once there, Grandma pulled two, small, white jewelry boxes out of her purse and laid them on the mat. They each had a rubber band wrapped around them to hold them closed. The huckster stepped behind the counter, half-smiled and half-smirked as he tenderly took off the top of the first box.

"Ahhh, coins, my favorite treasure. Let's examine what you have here," and then he began to take the coins out of the box very carefully, one at a time. He inspected the condition and date of each.

Grandma had an assortment of coins that she had collected from the time that she was a little girl. These were only a few of them. She had lots of pennies, nickels, and dimes, quarters, half dollars and silver dollars. All of her coins were minted before 1897, which was when she was born, and many of them were made of real silver, and a couple were real gold. You could tell that the swindler was very interested, because he was closely inspecting her coins as he wrote some notes.

The majority of his comments were, "Hhhhmmmm, uhh-huh, mmmmmmmm, uhh-huh, hhhhhmmmmm." In the end he said, "This is a very nice, sentimental collection Madame, but sadly it's not very valuable. I'm prepared to offer you five dollars above the face value of the coins in your collection." He said as he put the lid back on the box, acting somewhat disinterested.

I bristled at his offer. Sensing my anger, Grandma put her hand on my shoulder, smiled at the man very politely and said, "That's very generous sir, would you look at my box of stamps also please?"

What is she trying to do, I thought? She should know that he is trying to cheat her. She and I had checked the value of one of the silver dollars at the library. It was worth fifty dollars by itself. Why would she simply ask him about the stamps?

"Happily Madam, happily," he replied tapping his fingers together again. You could tell by his manner that he was feeling more and more confident, as he took the lid off of the small white box of stamps.

Grandma's stamps were old too. They didn't have any dates, and some of them only cost a penny or two each, but they were as old as her coins and they had large numbers or pictures of George Washington, Abraham Lincoln and Ben Franklin. I had never checked their values with Grandma at the library, but she said that she thought they were pretty valuable too.

After briskly looking at her stamps and mumbling, "Ttsskk, tsskkk, hhmmmmm," he mumbled, "Sadly Madame, your stamps aren't even as valuable as your coins. I could perhaps give you another two dollars for your stamps, if you sell them with your coins. Together you would have a tidy little sum to take home," he said with a big toothy smile.

Well with that final insult, I was ready to bop that bandit right where he stood, when Grandma gently squeezed my shoulder and said while she pointed behind the counter, "That's a very interesting camera. Is it one of the new ones that makes an instant picture?"

"Why yes, yes it is Madame. It's a Polaroid Land camera. We use it to take pictures of interesting coins and stamps that come in to the store."

"My goodness, well I never. May I see it work? Would you take a photo of my grandson?" and with that Grandma positioned me against some shelves so he could take my picture.

"Well, uuhh, I guess I could," he said with furrowed eyebrows. Then he seemed to think about it a second and

73

said quite assuredly, "Well yes, of course I could," he smiled even wider this time.

I was having a difficult time understanding what was happening and had a hard time being happy enough to have my photo taken.

"Stand up nice and tall young man and smile. On the count of three, 1—2—3," and with that the camera flashed, and he began a long-winded speech about how the camera worked. After he pulled the piece of film out of the back of the camera, we watched the photograph magically change from a piece of blank paper into a photograph of me.

It looked like a miracle. Then, with a flourish he said, "Voila Madame, a handsome photograph of your grandson!" and then he presented her with my photograph, which she scrutinized quite carefully.

"Well that is a miracle, isn't it sir? But, I wonder, no I hate to even mention it, but could you possibly take another photograph? He didn't do a very good job of smiling. Would you please?" and with that Grandma stood me up against a different set of shelves that looked more interesting as a background. As she inspected me carefully, she pulled my St. Christopher miraculous medal out from under my shirt and gently displayed it so it could be seen.

She winked at me and said, "Now this time Mickey, please give this nice man a very big smile, when he takes your picture." Then she stepped away, looked at the man and said, "He's ready."

"Yes, yes of course Madame. Stand up nice and tall young man and smile on the count of three, 1—2—3," and with that the camera flashed again, and he looked rather pleased with himself as we all watched my photograph magically appear, again. Then Grandma scrutinized it carefully yet again. In the end, she pronounced, "Better, it's much better. You did a very good job of smiling that time Mickey."

I was confused. Didn't she know that crook was trying to steal her coins and stamps? The man looked relieved that he wasn't required to take yet a third photo. Grandma put both photographs of me in her purse and then snapped it shut.

"Well these photographs are excellent sir, you are very kind. Thank you very much, I'll cherish them forever," and with that she grabbed her boxes off the counter, put their rubber bands on, grabbed my arm and said, "Come along Mickey, we've got much too much to do to waste any more of this fine man's time today."

'But, but," he blustered, "What about the coins and stamps Madame, aren't you going to sell them to me?"

"Of course not my dear man, they mean much too much to me to sell them, but thank you for your very generous offer," and in a flash we were headed down the thumping escalator.

When we were halfway down the escalator she said, "I don't know about you Mickey, but I'm famished. Let's go to Woolworth's for some lunch. I love to eat at their lunch counter. Don't you?"

"Well yeah, I do," I stammered, "but what about that crook? He was trying to steal your coins and stamps." Grandma just smiled.

"Why whatever do you mean Mickey? He was positively a saint and so courteous. Now we each have a photograph to remember this day."

I smiled too, in admiration of her. She'd just bested that man, and showed him who was boss without being nasty or insulting. It's not possible to love anyone more than I loved her at that moment. She was my hero.

"I wish my picture was of you Grandma."

"Well perhaps we'll visit him again sometime and see if he will take my photograph," she laughed.

The rest of the day was a blur of activity. We walked over to Woolworth's for lunch at the counter and then we walked east past Broadway towards the riverfront, so Grandma could show me where the Gateway Arch was being built. After gawking at the Arch's grounds, I saw the SS Admiral docked nearby. I yearned to be on it chugging up and down the muddy Mississippi playing nickel games and doing the Hokey Pokey.

We took the Broadway bus down to the Soulard Farmers' Market. At the Market Grandma demonstrated her negotiation and haggling skills again and again with every vendor that tried to sell her something. She was always able to 'squeeze' an extra lemon, tomato, or apple from every vendor before she agreed on the price. Then slowly, she inspected each piece of produce before she put it in the shopping bags, which she had me carry. I never realized how clever and smart she was until I observed Grandma in downtown that day.

Finally, after we visited what seemed like every produce, meat and bread stall in the Market, we climbed onto the Bi-State bus loaded with bags of groceries and headed back to Grandma's house. We didn't play our game of guessing peoples' lives, because I leaned my head on her shoulder and fell asleep before the bus pulled away from the curb. It was a Saturday to remember for sure.

Sunday morning after Mass at St. Joan of Arc Catholic Church, we headed to Uncle Bill's Pancake House in the Ol' Gray Mare. Grandma wanted to take me there to eat breakfast before she drove me home to my house. She knew I loved pancakes, and Uncle Bill's sign claimed he had 36 flavors of syrup and "All you can eat pancakes." I had bragged all morning about how I was going to taste each flavor of syrup and I told our waitress, Kathy, as soon as we were seated in our comfy red upholstered booth.

First, I gulped down a large glass of orange juice, then, Kathy brought our first batch of steaming hot pancakes to the table. I had already selected syrups for my first plate of pancakes. Each table had a spinning tray on it, which held 12 different bottles of syrup, but ours only had six. Kathy told me she would find a different tray, when I was ready for my next 12 flavors.

"Mickey, you don't have to taste every flavor of syrup for me," Grandma said, "Maybe you should just try six or seven today. We can come back another time to try some of the others."

"I know Grandma, but I really want to try all of them today. I'm a big kid now," I said.

"Well alright," she said reluctantly, "What's your first flavor?"

"I'm going try a different flavor of syrup on each pancake because their pancakes ain't too big. I'm starting with my favorite, blueberry. My last pancake is going to be maple because I've tasted it already."

I started with real gusto and polished off my blueberry pancake in a couple of bites. Next, I ate strawberry followed by boysenberry, chocolate, vanilla and grape, which surprisingly, tasted awful.

I ordered my second plate of pancakes and another tray of syrup from Kathy. Grandma was full so she did not order any more pancakes. I didn't want to tell Grandma that I was already feeling kind of full—but when she suggested that I try two flavors on each pancake, I jumped on her idea and acted like it was no big deal.

"Well, if you want me to, I will Grandma. After all, you're paying."

The second plate of pancakes took a little more time to eat than the first. I consoled myself with the fact that I was eating 12 more syrups instead of six, which gave me a total of 18 flavors tasted—half down and half to go. The flavors I tasted on the second plate were apple, orange, tangerine, lemon, grapefruit, cheesecake, pineapple, cherry, blackberry, peach, raspberry, and gooseberry, which was the sourest of all the syrups.

Kathy had been pointing to me and telling everyone in the restaurant what I was going to do. Everybody in the restaurant clapped and looked surprised, when I finished my second plate. Grandma looked worried, so I assured her with my smile of sublime confidence.

"Maybe you should stop Mickey. Twelve pancakes and 18 flavors are a lot for one boy to eat. I'm sure there's never been a boy your age that has eaten so much. Why don't you just sit there a minute and rest while I finish my hot tea. Then we'll leave."

"No way Grandma, I can't quit now. I'm just getting going," I lied. My stomach ached and it felt two sizes too small. I loosened my belt two notches. I had no idea how I could eat anymore. I didn't even feel comfortable moving in our booth.

"May I please have some more pancakes and syrup Kathy?

"You bet, Honey!" and with that she breezed into the kitchen.

To Grandma's chagrin, a customer in the restaurant was collecting bottles of syrup from the other tables to make sure that I had all 36 flavors available.

As my last plate of pancakes was delivered, Grandma came up with a swell idea.

"Why don't you put a different flavor of syrup on each bite of your pancakes Mickey, and maybe you won't get so full."

"Okay, Grandma, if you think that's best," I kind of half moaned praying that I could eat 18 more bites of pancakes. As I sat staring at my new stack of steaming pancakes with hot butter dripping down its sides, I unsnapped my pants and got serious about eating.

The first bite of my last plate of pancakes was lime syrup—yuck, next was coconut—which was okay, then butterscotch—too sweet, caramel—was sweeter than butterscotch, and then I gagged, which caused me to belch so loudly, everybody in the restaurant heard me. Grandma blanched. The man collecting the syrups for me laughed and howled "Good one, kid," as he slapped me on the back. I choked my way through small bites of coffee, banana, cinnamon, honey, molasses, raisin, mint, and apricot. After apricot, I stopped to catch my breath and see if my food would settle.

I took deep breaths and closed my eyes as I tried not to look at the pancakes and syrup for a few minutes. Just the thought of something sweet made me gag. I stood up next to our booth and stretched my arms above my head trying to make room in my stomach—it didn't help. I was so full, I thought my stomach would bust wide open. My belly looked like a ripe watermelon.

Grandma looked at me anxiously and asked, "Don't you think you've had enough Mickey?"

"I can't quit now, I'm almost done. Don't worry Grandma. I'm fine," I groaned but I could hardly smile.

I wondered if I could eat all 36 flavors. I had one and a half pancakes left on my plate.

A lot of people in the restaurant were standing around our booth. A couple of men were standing on their chairs to see well. Luckily we were sitting next to the outside window because some of the customers had even gone outside to watch me through the large plate glass window. They couldn't get close enough to me inside the restaurant to see really well.

As I picked up my fork, the man who had complimented my belch earlier, picked up a bottle of syrup from the line that he had created of the remaining flavors. Grandly he announced, "Praline," as he poured a dollop on the corner of my pancake. I appreciated his help. I took the bite, which was way too sweet.

I was running out of energy from being so full. Next, he announced, "Black Cherry." It was way too sweet too. Black Cherry was followed by "Date," which, thankfully, wasn't as sweet.

I was down to half of a pancake and two flavors of syrup—marshmallow and maple. Marshmallow was very, very sweet and very, very sticky. I was barely able to choke it down. As my last bite paused in front of my mouth, some of the men played a drum roll on the tables and booths with their hands. Everybody, inside and outside of the restaurant clapped as I reluctantly put the last bite into my mouth. Maple tasted awful too, but I usually liked it. I barely chewed before I swallowed, and swore that I would never eat another pancake for the rest of my life. To swallow, I stifled another belch, which I am sure would have caused me to puke. The crowd went wild with jubilation.

There was so much clapping and congratulating, you would have thought Stan Musial had hit another home run. Everybody was clapping and patting me on the back telling me, "Great job, Champ!" "I knew you would do it! You were so determined." When Grandma tried to pay our bill, the manager resisted and insisted that our meals were "Free, on the house!"

My stomach sloshed as I stumbled out of our booth and through the restaurant door. Grandma put on her nurse's face and quietly asked, "How do you feel Mickey?" She looked very worried.

"Full, Grandma, really full," I said as I tried to smile. My stomach hurt so badly I couldn't think. I walked like I was barefoot in broken glass; I didn't want to make any movement that would shake my stomach up.

"I'm never going to eat another pancake for the rest of my life Grandma," I quietly whimpered.

"I should wonder, but I guess you've learned a valuable lesson. Why it'd serve them right if..." and with that, I let go with a gut wrenching blast of Technicolor puke right there in the middle of Uncle Bill's parking lot. It was the kind of mess that the porter would have to clean up with a hose and lots of water.

As we drove home, my stomach stopped churning and I started feeling better. Although I was sad that our weekend was ending, the din of all the car horns tooting at us made me smile as I sat looking at the photograph Grandma had given me to remind me of our special adventure together. There I was standing in the Famous-Barr store smiling with my St. Christopher medal displayed.

Chapter 5

Bloody Red Badges of Courage

Every boy thinks of himself as a courageous, strong, virile, and dashing superhero just like Superman or John Wayne as soon as he can walk in or on his dad's shoes.

Therefore, it is only natural that boys should brag about the same things that men brag about. A boy brags about his hair, his beard, his good looks, how big his muscles are, how smart he is, how fast he can run, how high he can jump, and who he can beat up. If he's a total failure, he brags about how much stuff his parents have. However, the bragging stories that top all others are the stories about courage and guts.

Boys measure other boys' courage, and their own, by bragging about the number and nature of scars and injuries they have achieved by displaying their manhood. Learning how to brag without sounding too boastful is an art. It's called the humble brag. The trick is to appeal for a little extra credit and admiration from your buddies without sounding so bodacious that you get accused of lying. Once you are caught in an outright lie or an extravagant elaboration you will lose "courage" credibility quickly and possibly forever.

Men have sat in sacred circles of camaraderie for millennia debating and recounting the relative values of various feats of bravery and heroism. The lively debates, which can quickly turn into ferocious arguments, try to establish the credibility of someone's claims about his manliness. This tribal process or "parley" insures a historical and factual representation of the event rather than an "artistic or fictional" interpretation.

Eyewitnesses are very valuable during this parley, which is why you always hear boys yell things like, "Look at me! I'm over here! Look! I'm hanging by one arm from this tree branch, which is hanging over a deep, muddy creek that's full of diphtheria germs and water-moccasin snakes! Look at me!"

Witnesses are more valuable than soda bottles with a two-cent deposit, when you need someone to attest to your lion-hearted legends of courage and valor. Witnesses can testify to your unshrinking fearlessness, but a witness's report is suspicious if the witness is your best friend.

There is only one thing better than having an eyewitness who is a neutral disbeliever—you have to have a jagged and angry looking scar. Ugly, raised, nasty looking purple-red scars stand in silent testament and witness to man's bold acts of bravery and courage.

Scars are rock solid undeniable evidence that proclaims you are spirited and unafraid—a real "man's man." It's also important to note that sometimes it's best not to have eyewitnesses, when you receive some form of vicious physical or psychological trauma. With any good luck at all, your trauma will result in a nice colorful ugly scar, but the bad luck of having a witness can be testament to your hysterics, panic, and bawling while and after you received this epic and whopping trauma.

This is why boys, and men, are less careful than they should be about protecting their bodies from injury and harm, and why bodily scars are so useful and helpful. Who can argue about your bravery and strength, when you can clearly point to a hideous and ghastly scar prominently showcased on your body? Nobody.

An honor council parley that reviews and awards rank for bravery is called to order when someone makes an appeal to document an event or injury that demonstrates his bravery and courage. The person presenting the event wants his record of bravery reviewed by the group for a possible promotion in his social status. At least that was Rod's intention as he approached us at the Clubhouse this afternoon.

We were all bored and just hanging out at the Clubhouse trying to think of something to do with the rest of a sunny Saturday afternoon, when Rod arrived. Rod had been rainbow trout fishing at Bennett Springs State Park with his dad and older brothers the weekend before. I have never been fishing so I was impressed by the fact that Rod knew how to fish, and fishing for trout raised his credibility level to "exotic" with me but not with some of the other guys.

"What's up guys? How are you doing?" asked an eager and smiling Rod as he approached us. Rod was wearing a new baseball cap with a patch that said, 'Bennett Springs State Park.' It even had a colorful rainbow trout embroidered on it.

"Hey Rod! How was your vacation?" I asked.

"Aww geez, it was great! I had a lot of fun until," and then he gave a long pause for effect. "Well, I don't want to talk about it though," he said stopping for a moment to think while he grimaced. "It was great fishing with Dad and my brothers. We caught a lot of rainbow trout."

Rod's stealthy subterfuge was fairly transparent. Pausing to suggest some unspeakable and potentially horrific event during his vacation was a clever ploy to pique all of our interests and begin an impromptu tribal review of his record for bravery. Maybe he had seen a ghost, fallen into a well or been bitten by a wolf. I fell for his ploy, hook, line and sinker.

"What happened Rod?" I asked.

"Aww, I don't want to talk about it Mickey. It was nothing—really, it was nothing," as he slowly shook his head, leaving the impression of ghastly memories.

Slowly he took off his forest green Bennett Springs ball cap, which carefully exposed his left arm to our view.

"Something must have happened Rod, tell us," I pleaded swallowing his baited comment.

"Well, okay," he sighed, resigning himself to the fact that he would have to recount all of the grisly details to satisfy our aroused curiosities.

"See this?" he asked pointing to a place on the inside of his left wrist just above the palm of his hand. We all jumped and shoved each other out of the way to get close so we had a good view of his forearm that had been extended towards us so we could easily see.

"Where?' Tommy asked, cynically scrunching up his eyes for better focus, "I don't see anything. What're you talking about? There ain't anything there but some freckles."

"There is too, look!" pleaded Rod, a little too anxiously.

"I see it," said Dave, "I think," questioning himself as he screwed his eyeballs closer to Rod's arm.

"Right there," declared Rod pointing to a couple of small red spots that looked suspiciously like mosquito bites. We were immediately suspicious of Rod's fish story.

"Well tell us what happened Rod," demanded Joey as he formally convened Rod's review of courage and bravery with a slap on his knee.

Rod started his tale cautiously like he didn't want to recall the horrible things that had happened to him. "Well," he droned, as he sensed the need to choose his words very, very carefully lest we accuse him of bragging or worse yet—lying, "When we were at Bennett Springs Dad taught me to noodle fish."

"Noodle fish?" I asked, "There's fishes called noodles? I haven't heard of any noodle fishes before. Have you guys? What's a noodle fish look like Rod?"

"I didn't say I fished for any noodle fish Mickey," sounding a little too exasperated. " I said, Dad took me noodle fishing."

"Well, that's what I just said Rod. Can't you speak good English? You said you went... whatchamacallit—trout fishing didn't you?"

"Yeah," he said looking worn out with his confidence fading.

"What's the difference between trout fishing and noodle fishing? They sound the same to me Rod. You're either fishing for trouts or you're fishing for noodles. It's not my fault you're confusing your stories or *changing* them." I emphasized the word 'changing.'

"It sounds like he's lying to me too Mickey," said Tommy very quickly, while he cynically arched his eyebrow for effect and gave a hard, scrutinizing stare at Rod's arm. Tommy acted like he was a Supreme Court justice or someone really important like a suspicious mother.

Rod knew his honor review was going poorly, and he sounded somewhat panicky, when he said, "Noodle fishing is when you catch catfish with your hands. You don't use a fishing pole or a hook."

"Are you saying you don't use a fishing pole to catch a catfish Rod?" I asked staying on the attack and angling to enhance my own credibility with a critical line of penetrating questions. Tommy nodded his head to show his agreement with my line of questions.

"Right Mickey, you don't use a pole. You use your hands," he said holding and waving his barely marked left hand high in the air.

"Never?" I asked.

"Well you can use a pole for catfish, but not when you're noodle fishing. You use your hand, when you noodle fish."

"Fishing is way too confusing to me. Did you catch a catfish or not," asked Joey sounding more than a little frustrated with the proceedings and attempting to cut to the facts.

"Yeah," said Rod.

"With your hands?" I asked harshly.

"Yeah," said Rod hopefully. "That's how I got bit on my arm," he said holding his arm up in the air again.

"That ain't no bite mark," said Tommy mockingly. "When I got bit by Bobby's dog, he bit right through my jeans and there were bloody holes in my leg and everything. I even had to get a tetanus shot. Did you get a tetanus shot Rod? Did you have to see a doctor?"

"No," said Rod sounding totally defeated and wishing he'd kept his mouth shut and not said a word.

"Then you couldn't have been bit by any catfish, noodle fish or any other kind of fish either," declared Tommy with a "Hurrumph," as he crossed his arms triumphantly. He was proud that he had introduced his crucial medical evidence about the tetanus shot and doctor visit.

I agreed with Tommy's assessment. Rod's story sounded really fishy to me too and his look of dejection and defeatism told that story. I was hoping the court of review was going to deny Rod's appeal for higher status for conspicuous courage under fire.

Tommy's critical cross-examination served yet another purpose. He had opened the Court of Appeals, and Tommy's case was first.

"Tommy, how many holes did you have in your leg from Bobby's dog?" asked Billy.

"Two, but they were deep and they wouldn't quit bleeding," replied Tommy, "I almost had to get stitches."

"Did you ever get stitches?" asked Rod hoping for a reprieve. "I did. I got four of them right here in my knee," he said pointing to a small crescent-moon shaped scar on his right knee.

"That's nothing," said Billy, after his trick question to Tommy that opened his own appeal for higher status.

"Look at this!" he said proudly pointing to his left elbow. "When I broke my arm playing football," he said beaming with pride, "the broken bone came right through my skin, and the Doc had to push the bone back in and sew me up. I got 24 stitches."

It was true. The long and jagged scar on Billy's left elbow always impressed anybody who saw the ghastly scar. He rarely wore a long-sleeve shirt even in the winter, so that it was easy for everybody to see his jagged medal of honor, courage and bravery.

I bit my lip and shook my head after Billy's story because I knew what was coming. I remembered the day, when we were all playing football and Billy broke his arm. Dave had toppled Billy with a courageous shoe-top tackle while Billy was running with the football for a sure touchdown. Billy slammed hard into the trunk of an old elm tree that marked the out-of-bounds. The old Elm snapped Billy's strong arm like a piece of kindling wood. Since Billy was bigger, stronger and older than Dave, you can bet Dave never let Billy forget that he had broken Billy's arm. Dave's rough and tough tackle was honored as highly as Billy's scar, and we were all witnesses to both accomplishments.

"Yeah, you sure did Billy," mocked Dave to Billy's embarrassment, "And' I'll break your other arm, if you mess with me." Dave sat there smiling like he knew something that none of us knew.

"Well come on then Dave," said Billy, jumping to his feet and putting up his fists like he was going to duke it out with Dave right then and there, "Let's see you break my arm now, you lucky little leprechaun. You didn't break my arm, the tree did."

"Get out of here," said Dave waving off Billy's challenge, "I don't want to make you cry again, you big cry baby!"

No question. Dave's taunt had crossed the line of fairness, and Billy's temper was quick to boil. We were all playing football that day, when we heard the bone in Billy's arm snap. After he slammed into the tree, we heard him bawl like a baby. He cried loud and hard all the way to his house, and he cried while his mom and dad packed him into the family's white Ford station wagon to take him to St. Joseph's emergency room in downtown St. Charles. We all knew that we would have been crying too. So, when Billy jumped on Dave and put him into a full-nelson headlock, while he wrestled him to the ground, and pushed Dave's face in the dust nobody was feeling too sorry for Dave. He'd gone too far.

"How do you like these rotten apples Dave? Are you going to break my arm now?" chided Billy, while Dave spit dust and tried to scramble from under Billy's much larger body.

"Say uncle, and I'll let you up you little twerp," said Billy showing his benevolence.

"Never," growled Dave as he spit dust out of his mouth and blew it out of his nose. "You're going to have to kill me first," declared Dave as he wiggled and writhed under Billy's weight to no avail.

"Come on," said Billy, "I don't want to hurt you Dave. Just say uncle," pleaded Billy already regretting that he had started this wrestling match.

Dave was the smallest guy in our group, yet we all knew he would never surrender. He was as tough as a knot in a board. For this to end, Billy would have to kill Dave or surrender to Dave. Neither seemed very likely. While Billy sat on top of Dave's chest pinning his arms with his knees, Billy pleaded for Dave's capitulation. Dave bucked Billy like a bronco.

As we waited for a final decision on the wrestling match, Tommy said, "Well, I have a lot more than 24 stitches if you add them up. I've got five stitches in my head from the swing set, four in the bottom of my foot, when I stepped on the broken bottle, and four more in my hand, when I fell on that tree root at the rope swing down at the creek. How many is that?"

"Thirteen," declared Billy adjusting his grip on Dave so he couldn't squirm as much, "Say uncle Dave!"

"Never!" said Dave defiantly.

Tommy had done me a favor by changing the criteria and strategy for an honor council review. In the past, we reviewed one incident of bravery at a time to determine a boy's courage. Tommy presented his total number of stitches as a comprehensive package to the council for review. In other words, a total of thirteen stitches over three injuries. This new add-them-up strategy could be very helpful to me. I was always getting hurt and I figured it was time to get some credit for all of my injuries lumped together.

"I got bit by Bobby's dog and Pete's dog too—and I got whatchamacallit, tetanus shots each time," I said pleading to the gang for some recognition and reconsideration.

"Well Pete's little brother bit you on the butt too. Didn't you get a tetanus shot for that?" added Tommy.

"No, but I got a tetanus shot, when that rusty nail went through the sole of my Keds at the park," I countered. "They were afraid I'd get lockjaw. And, remember when I fell off my bike and cut my hand so bad I had to wear a bandage for a week?" My stories of courage were gathering steam, "and when I chipped my tooth roller skating, and when I fell on the steps and cut my forehead? I got 12 stitches."

"Aww, those are little kid hurts Mickey, they're not like having a compound fracture of your arm," scoffed

Billy, "I had to wear a cast for months and they put pins in my arm too—*SAY UNCLE DAVE*!" yelled Billy.

"*NEVER*—but I'm going to break your other arm," screamed an agitated, irate and dusty-faced Dave, "if you don' let me up—*RIGHT NOW*," yelled Dave with spit coming out of his mouth.

"No Dave, you have to say uncle first," said Billy, as he grappled to keep control of Dave's arms.

"Well," I said, feeling underappreciated, "I've been hurt more than anybody else here."

"Just because your accident prone, don't mean nothing Mickey," said Rod. "We all got little kid hurts as much as you, but we have gotten manly hurts too. You haven't."

That remark smarted, so I hopped up and was ready to thrash Rod, but Joey kept us apart and said, "You been hurt just as much as us Mickey. Don't let Rod work you up. He's mad because nobody thinks much of his noodle bite, that's all."

"I am not," claimed Rod, "and I didn't get bit by no noodle. It was a 30-pound catfish!"

"Are too," I said.

"Okay," said Billy feeling frustrated and bored, "I'm going to let you up Dave. Just remember I was nice to you and don't mouth off no more."

"I will if I want," said Dave as Billy climbed off of his chest and clambered to his feet to strut away.

"Let's see if we can sneak into those new duplexes they're building on Tropic Drive by the St. Ann ballpark," suggested Joey as he treaded off towards the park.

"Okay," everybody agreed as we walked next to each other exchanging jibes and laughing—even Rod. Everyone had forgotten the court of honor except Dave, who was lurking behind us. His pride was hurt and his face and clothes were dusty.

Then faster than a speeding bullet, Dave sprinted toward Billy's back and tackled him hard from behind. Billy hit the hard dusty ground face first like a sack of potatoes. There was a loud thud as Billy gasped and swallowed a mouthful of dust.

Dave ran off laughing, and as he did he said, "I told you, I'd get you back Billy!"

Luckily, Billy didn't break either of his arms, legs or skull and he was able to jump up quickly. He slapped the dust out of his blue jeans and white t-shirt, while he yelled, "Dang you Dave! I should've known you'd do it. Next time, I'm not going to be nice to you and let you up!"

Quietly, we all smiled. We admired Dave's courage. Billy laughed to himself as he slapped the dust out of his jeans and muttered something about leprechauns. Size didn't matter. Dave was the smallest guy, but he was as tough as a piece of oak, and oddly, he didn't have any scars that I had ever seen.

Chapter 6

Starr's Satellites &
Suzie's Tomatoes

It was the first day of summer. We were out of school, and I figured that I was on vacation for the entire summer. Just like Christmas vacation, or Easter vacation, I didn't differentiate from the days I spent at home during the summer and the time that we traveled to visit our relatives. Vacation is vacation. I was on vacation for the entire three-months–Whoopee! Summer is my favorite vacation. It is sandwiched between Memorial Day and Labor Day, and I am ready for every bite. I have been planning what I am going to do during my summer vacation ever since my Easter vacation.

This summer I am going to explore a different stretch of Cold Water Creek, ride my bike to the American Legion Park Pool on Midland Road, go to the St. Ann Park summer day camp, do a campout in our clubhouse, cut grass to make some money, go on our family vacation to Indiana, play hide-and-seek until late at night, read comics, catch crawdads, hang out with my buddies, roller-skate, play Red-Rover, Statues and Capture the Flag, ride bikes, watch baseball games, and wake up early every day. The one thing that I plan to do the most this summer is play baseball.

We play baseball every day. In fact, we usually play baseball a couple of times every day. My friends and I play baseball every way a kid can play baseball.

We play in the streets with a tennis ball or a rubber ball, and use trees, chalk, manhole sewer covers, or our baseball gloves as our bases. We play on dirt fields with hardballs. We play in our yards with Wiffle balls, and we play in schoolyards with anything that is round including cork-balls and bottle caps. We hit all of these various orbs and objects with official wooden baseball bats, hollow plastic Wiffle ball bats, thin wooden cork-ball bats, and sawed-off broomstick handles that have been taped for better gripping. We play catch, grounders, hotbox, fuzz-ball, Indian ball, Wiffle ball, softball (only if we had to because we can't find any other balls), home run derby, and regular baseball games with dozens of guys. Then, when nobody else is around, we throw rubber balls and tennis balls against our steps for pop-ups or brick walls for line drives and fly balls. We like to play against Kroger's blonde brick walls because we can draw different color and sized squares and circles on it. The only time we play with adults around is when we play on our official Khoury League Baseball team.

The name of my Khoury League team is the 'Satellites' and the Satellites have won first place every year. We are a legend, and I was selected for the All-Star team the last two years as the catcher. I love playing catcher, and I love playing for the Satellites.

When the Satellites were first started, our uniforms were makeshift and rag-tag. Each guy wore a navy blue baseball cap with a white 'S' on it, a white t-shirt with the name of our sponsor, "Kraft's Miracle Lounge," written in blue on the back and front, and we wore our own blue jeans.

Last year one of the mothers found a good buy on some used white wool baseball pants with blue stripes, and blue stirrup baseball socks with white stripes, and of course we wore our dirty Keds, Converse, or PF Flyers tennis shoes. Our tennis shoes weren't really tennis shoes. They were all-sport, low-top or high-top canvas shoes with rubber-tread soles.

None of the Satellites' players have baseball spikes; we wear the kind of tennis shoes that are on sale at the Buster Brown shoe store. My parents buy me a new pair of tennis shoes every summer and I usually need a new pair by the fall. This summer I got a pair of low-top white Keds.

This year we hit the big time—Coach Starr found a rich sponsor for the Satellites, and the sponsor bought brand new uniforms for all of us. To say our parents were thrilled about the prospect of new uniforms would be an understatement. They were electrified by the fact that their sons were getting brand new uniforms, and that it wouldn't cost them a single red-plastic cent. The guys on the team were so excited; we were acting like we had ants in our pants.

Everybody's exhilaration was heightened by the suspense that no one had seen the new uniforms. Coach Starr is the only person who knows who our new sponsor is and what our new uniforms look like. Oh, there has been endless speculation since our practices started a month ago, but Coach won't tell a soul—not even his wife or son. It's not that we didn't ask. Everybody badgered Coach before, during, and after every practice, before church and after church, at the post office, at the grocery store, and everywhere else he crossed paths with his players, his assistant coaches, our parents, or his wife and young son. Coach Starr's mouth has been shut tighter than our parents' wallets. Nobody knows but Coach and the sponsor, and he isn't telling until he makes the announcement and gives out our uniforms at the team meeting—tonight!

We are meeting at St. Kevin's in the school cafeteria at 7:00 p.m.—sharp. The guys had gone to the school's ball field early. We rode our bikes and brought our gloves, bats, and balls so we can play before the meeting.

All of the Satellites' players are going into fifth grade at St. Kevin's school next fall. We have been playing ball as a team since we were in the first grade, and Coach Starr has always been our coach.

He is the best coach in Khoury League, but he is to put it politely—*different*. Some parents say "odd" and others say "eccentric," but everyone agrees he is "different."

As a younger man, Coach was a pitcher on a traveling fast-pitch softball team called the *All-Starrs*. There were only four players on his team and he was the best. He bragged that his *All-Starr's* had never lost a game, and that nobody had ever hit one of his fast-pitch softballs out of the infield. Everybody, including fathers, mothers, sons, daughters and opposing coaches had tried to hit one of his pitches. He always waved a crisp ten-dollar bill in front of everybody's face saying it was theirs—all they had to do was hit the softball—nobody ever did. Being a famous softball pitcher didn't make Coach "different." It was the uniform that he wore to every game that we played that made him "different."

He wore a silky red, white, and blue shirt that had glittery silver letters that spelled out his *All Starr's* team name on the front and a big white number one inside of a big red star embroidered on the back. What was really odd was his baseball pants. They were silky too, but they were bright green with bright yellow stripes on the sides. On his head, he would wear one of our Satellites ball caps. No doubt, he looked goofy, but nobody ever told him. I guess they were afraid he would challenge them to hit one of his pitches. He taught me to catch his pitching, and I loved being the catcher.

Everybody always told me that being the catcher is the hardest position to play. I don't know about the hardest, but it sure is the dirtiest and hottest, especially in July and August. I liked being the catcher for the Satellites for lots of reasons. I got to wear all of the cool catcher's equipment, throw the baseball more than anybody else, and watch everyone and everything the whole game. Most of all, I liked the fact that I got to talk as much as I wanted the entire game.

The catcher is the quarterback, and he gets to talk to his players. I got to tell my players how many outs the other team had, where to throw the ball to get the next out, and which player was supposed to take my throw if somebody tried to steal a base. I also got to tell the pitcher, which pitch to throw, and where to throw it. Finally, I got to talk to the umpires and the other team's batters the whole game.

I liked "razzing" the other team's batters by saying things so they'd swing at bad pitches and not swing at good pitches, but I had to be careful. Coach Starr insisted that his players and their parents demonstrate good sportsmanship. He would take you out of the game if you threw a bat or helmet, argued with the umpire, or blamed a teammate. I was always polite, but I played to win.

Like Coach Starr said, "Mickey, there's an art to chatter with the batter."

My secret was to act like the batter's best friend, from the moment he walked up to home plate to bat. I usually started by saying something like, "How is it going man?" or "What's up!" Then I would give the batter a real big smile meant to throw him off guard.

Batters expected catchers to be combative and bad mouth his team and how they were playing.

I wanted the batter to trust me. Every batter is nervous as he walks up to home plate, even Stan "The Man" Musial. The batter knows his coaches, teammates, fans, and parents all want him to get on base. So you better believe he's nervous as he tries to nod or mumble something back to me after I say hello. My chatter is meant to break his concentration.

After the batter meets me, the friendly catcher, his newest and best friend, who says hello and smiles, I offer him some friendly advice to help him get on base. With a sincere look, I might suggest, "Don't swing at his fastball. He's wild today," or "Don't swing at his curveball, it's nasty," or, "Don't let them (and then point to his fans in the stands, with my mask) get you nervous, just do your best, they won't be *too mad* if you make an out."

My personal favorite is when a batter swings and misses a pitch. I take off my mask and say with mock-sincerity, "Listen to me, I'll tell you, when to swing," and then I wink. That's when the batter listens to me just like I was his best friend.

When I am catching, my goal is to keep the batter nervous and confused. When he strikes out, I always tell him how sorry I am and wish him better luck the next time. You would be surprised at the number of guys that say, "Thanks Mickey," after they strike out. Now that is sportsmanship.

The entire Satellite team and fan base had gathered in St. Kevin's cafeteria to see and receive our new uniforms, which were sitting on the floor in large, unlabeled brown cardboard boxes behind Coach Starr. The boxes were taped shut so no one could peek inside. Our first game of the season was scheduled for this coming Saturday, so our new uniforms had arrived just in time.

I was sitting on the floor between our shortstop, Kevin, and our pitcher, Denny.

Coach was dressed in his colorful uniform, and as he began talking to the large crowd of Satellite fans, the only sound we heard was Frank's baby sister crying. Naturally, everyone turned toward the sound, so Frank's mom nervously carried the baby outside. When there was complete silence again, Coach Starr began talking—again.

After some nice compliments about how hard all of 'his boys' had been practicing this spring, Coach took plenty of time to talk about the new uniforms before he gave them out to the players.

"As everybody knows, this year the Satellites are going to be wearing the high quality uniforms that *my boys* deserve. My boys aren't wearing blue jeans anymore," and with that the attentive crowd broke into a cacophony of hurrahs, whoops and hollers.

After some long moments, Coach put both of his hands up in the air to quiet the crowd and then he continued, "As you all know, the Satellites have won every game we've played for the past two years— *WE'RE WINNERS!*" We broke into more hurrahs, whoops and hollers.

Again Coach held his hands up as Frank's mom and sister snuck back inside, "I decided this year that we deserved some new uniforms," more hurrahs, whoops and hollers from the fans all wearing and waving their blue Satellite baseball caps.

Coach held his hands up again, "The first thing I changed was our ball caps," and with that Coach pulled a brand new red baseball cap with a white 'S' embroidered on it out of a cardboard box and proudly placed it on his head with both hands like a crown.

There was a couple of gasps followed by a restrained silence before someone quietly asked, "What about our blue caps, Coach? The Satellites have always worn blue caps," and the crowd and I nodded our silent agreement.

"That's true," said Coach, "that's very true, but somebody tell me, are the Satellites *HOT* or cold?" [Long pause] "Well tell me are we *HOT* or cold?"

And in unison, the blue-capped crowd shouted, "*HOT* Coach, the Satellites are *HOT*!"

"That's right, the *SATELLITES ARE HOT*," he roared waving his hands in the air, "so we should wear *RED* ball caps, not blue, and besides, it's the same color the Cardinals wear!"

And with those simple explanations, everybody in the crowd knew Coach Starr was right, and that was why he was a great coach and the Satellites were a winning team. Red was the best color for the Satellites not blue, and the crowd's hurrahs, whoops, hollers and handclapping began all over again reaffirming the Coach's decision about red. Coach had to hold up his hands to signal for quiet—again. The crowd could hardly contain itself.

"Now, let me introduce all of 'my boys' for this year's Satellite team and give each one his *new RED ball cap*!" By the time Coach had introduced each of 'his boys' and gave each one of us a new red cap, I had clapped so hard and long that my hands were stinging and the same color as my new ball cap.

I wasn't sure how, but by the time the players were wearing our new red ball caps, the crowd had grown into a riotous frenzy. During the ceremony, Coach announced that he had extra red ball caps that families could purchase and wear to the games. The crowd clapped even louder.

It seemed strange to see the Satellites sitting in the sea of red ball caps that had moments before been blue. Some of the fathers preferred a bare head to their old faithful blue caps, which they had taken off. Me too, I was proudly wearing my red cap, after I took my Stan Musial baseball flip card out of my blue cap and put it in the headband of my new red ball cap. Carefully, I began bending the bill of my new cap so it didn't look too new. Strangely, it seemed like the Satellites had always worn red. We were so happy we were glowing.

As the color change to red took hold, someone shouted out, "What about the rest of the uniform, Coach? Are the boys going play in their skivvies and t-shirts?" After the laughs, hurrahs, whoops, and hollers, the handclapping was louder than ever before.

We were in frenzy, so with his hands held up pleading for quiet, Coach said, "Well I can see everyone's excited so let's get this show on the road!"

As he opened another box Coach said, "Since number six is right here on top, Mickey, why don't you come up here and help me show off these new uniforms. Would you?"

"Sssure Coach, I'd be proud to," I stammered as I stumbled up to where Coach was standing.

The first thing Coach had me do was take off my tennis shoes and slip on a pair of our new red with white stripe stockings. They had straps and slid right over my pair of white socks. They looked professional.

Some of the fans started to clap as Coach had me begin to slip on a pair of our new white flannel cotton baseball pants right over my blue jean shorts. The pants were plenty baggy and just short enough to show my red stockings. The best thing about the baseball pants though was that they had a red stripe going up the outside of each pant leg, and they had a red belt too. As I looked down at myself, I thought that I looked like a real ball player. I felt great and so did everybody looking at me.

The only thing I needed was my uniform's shirt, as I stood facing the audience. From behind me, Coach slipped my shirt on over my white t-shirt. Right on the left breast was my lucky number '6.' Like the pants, the uniform shirt had red piping around the sleeves, the neck and the buttons. As I buttoned and tucked in my shirt, I heard some gasps from some awestruck fans. Not only was this the nicest uniform we had ever worn, it was the nicest uniform any Khoury League team had ever worn.

Coach was right—red was our color, and I looked good in it. Everyone was clapping and I couldn't wait until our baseball season started.

After the ooohhs and aaahhs, Phil's mom said, "Coach, these uniforms must have cost the sponsor a fortune. They're beautiful!"

"Well you're right Mary Margaret, they are handsome and very expensive. We are very lucky to have such generous sponsor, and the sponsor deserves a big round of applause right now!"

And that triggered everybody to clap so hard his or her hands stung and turned a deeper shade of red.

"Coach, who's our mystery sponsor, the Millionaire? *"The Millionaire"* is a television series where an unseen millionaire gives away his money to people who need it. Everybody laughed.

"Well no, he's not The Millionaire. Mickey would you please turn around so everyone can read our sponsor's name on the back of your uniform shirt?" I was happy to oblige so I turned around as quick as I could.

I didn't hear anything. There was absolute silence. Nobody said a word or emitted a sound. Then I heard Ronny's little sister ask, "Mommy, does that say, Suzie's Tomatoes? Is Mickey one of Suzie's Tomatoes Mommy?"

"Quiet dear. I don't know," said Ronny's mom.

There was more stunned silence and I felt my face glowing as red as my hat. I wondered what that little girl meant when she said Suzie's Tomatoes.

I didn't understand her question. Did she say that my uniform said Suzie? What the heck did Suzie's Tomatoes mean? I never heard of them before. Quickly, I turned around to face the crowd and see what was happening. Everybody's jaws were agape. They were struck speechless and stupefied like the Wizard of Oz witch had cast a nasty spell on them.

Toby's dad, Mr. Clarke, shouted, "Turn around again Mickey," and I quickly obliged and faced the blank wall.

"Who the hell is Suzie's Tomatoes Coach? Ooops. Excuse my French folks, but what in Sam Hill are we going to do?" asked Mr. Clarke.

"Suzie's Tomatoes is our new sponsor, Tom. They paid for Toby's and all of the boys' uniforms and all of our new catching and batting equipment too. That's who the heck Suzie's Tomatoes is."

"I've never heard of them, Coach," said Mr. Bitters.

"We haven't either," said Mister and Missus Homily.

"Well you have now Peter, Paul and Mary. Suzie's Tomatoes just paid 20 bucks for each uniform you see. So everybody here should go buy some of Suzie's Tomatoes at the Kroger or A&P grocery stores first thing tomorrow," said Coach.

"Yeah, but Coach, shouldn't Suzie's Tomatoes be a sponsor for a girls' softball team instead of a boys' championship baseball team?"

"Why? Should your girl's uniform look better than your boy's, George?" countered Coach with a laugh.

Feeling a little unnerved by what I was hearing, I took off my shirt so I could take a look at the back of it for myself. There it was, bright as day it said, Suzie's

Tomatoes. The red words were written in a girly-looking script and the words covered the entire back of my uniform shirt. I was dumbstruck.

How could Coach find a sponsor named Suzie's Tomatoes? I thought. I looked at the guys on the team, and they were all sitting there in their new ball caps that were the color of a tomato looking dejected and glum. The thrill was gone and nobody was smiling. We sat there confused, and we felt betrayed somehow.

We were happy to have such good looking and professional uniforms, but we were sad because they said, Suzie's Tomatoes. Slowly, I put my new uniform shirt back on and looked at the great Stan Musial's number '6' over my heart and heaved a baffled sigh.

Then, out of nowhere Jack Junior, his teammates called him J.J., shouted, "Mickey, you look like a bottle of ketchup and that 'S' on your hat stands for Sissies—Suzie's Sissies!"

Evidently, Jack Junior had been spying in the back of the cafeteria all evening, and he ran out the cafeteria door laughing hysterically. Over his shoulder, he screamed, "See you on the field you bunch of sissies!"

Several of the guys chased him, but he had already jumped on his black Schwinn racer and sped away before the guys could catch him.

Jack Junior's dad was the coach of the *V.F.W. Rebels*, our archrivals. We called him Jack Junior because his dad was Jack Kline, senior. Although we were the first place team in our league, the Rebels always had the best looking uniforms and they almost beat us every time we played. The scores of our games were always very close. The Rebels uniforms were dark gray with red pin stripes and yellow piping. *V.F.W. Rebels* was written across the front of their uniform shirts and their numbers were written large on the back. Their caps were gray with red bills and a red 'R' was embroidered on it. Mr. Kline tried to recruit me to play with the Rebels every year, but I always stayed with Coach and the Satellites. Now, I kind of wished I were the catcher for the Rebels and not Suzie's Tomatoes.

We needed a sponsor like the V.F.W. The Veterans of Foreign Wars sponsored teams at every age level of Khoury League and their teams always came in first, every team that is, except the Rebels. They were always second behind the Satellites, but I was beginning to wonder if the Rebels would win first place this year. In my head, I could hear Jack Junior and his dad laughing out loud about our new uniforms.

It was going to be a very long baseball season.

Chapter 7

Midsummer Night's Skullduggery

Our lives changed forever, the day Joey stayed home from school acting sick. I remember walking into our house after school and being grabbed and pulled downstairs to the secret closet under the basement steps by Joey. It was our favorite secret hiding spot.

"Look," he said proudly as he unfolded a large sheet of white butcher paper that he had gotten from the Kroger store. It had a detailed architectural rendering of a four-story clubhouse that included separate bedrooms for him and me. We shared a bedroom now so that was really cool.

"Are we running away?" I asked innocently.

"No, it's a clubhouse we're going build," he said, and we did. Maybe it wasn't as grand and spacious as his first drawing, but we spent one whole Christmas vacation building the "Clubhouse." Dad and our neighbor Frank helped too. All of the guys that helped build it in the below-freezing weather became members of our secret club, the "Pirates."

The Pirates was a small exclusive club. The only requirement to be a member was that you had to have helped build the Clubhouse. Joey swore us all to secrecy, and none of our other friends knew we were the Pirates. Only Pirates knew other Pirates. Our other friends and kids in the neighborhood saw our Jolly Roger Pirate flags, when we left them around the neighborhood. No one knew who the Pirates were. We were a secret club.

Joey was our captain, and he had called the Pirates' 'first of the summer' special meeting for tonight. We were all busy collecting our stuff for our campout in the Clubhouse.

The Pirates had two campouts last summer, and we wanted more this summer. Our parents were hesitant to give their permissions because of something that happened last summer. This year, our moms and dads were watching us like prison guards.

We didn't get caught doing anything last summer; it's just that our parents thought they had caught us doing something last summer.

Last summer, our parents had found out a group of boys was spotted and chased by cops in their cruisers with their lights flashing. The boys were seen roaming our neighborhood streets in the middle of the night.

None of us were caught. A Pirate's flag had been found by one of the cops lying on the ground.

On that very same night, we had camped out in the Clubhouse. There was no proof that we had done anything so we were declared innocent, but our parents were very, very suspicious, and we knew we had to be very, very careful.

The Pirates quickly became a neighborhood legend. None of us knew what Joey had in mind for tonight, but we were ready for anything.

We could not bring too many supplies into the Clubhouse because it was not as big as Joey's dream house. It was one room and pretty cramped. All of the guys slept head-to-toe on the floor, but one of us could sleep in the attic loft if we needed the extra space. In addition, there was a lookout deck above the roof that made room for another one or two guys to sleep outside under the stars. It was not huge, but it was ours and our parents couldn't fit in the front door very easily to look at our stuff.

The lookout was Dave's and my favorite place to sleep. Since I was the fastest and Dave was the second fastest, we were the Pirates' scouts. Sleeping on top of the Clubhouse was perfect for us. There was a railing around the lookout deck so we couldn't roll off and a ladder that we could pull up. It allowed us to get off of the lookout deck without going into the Clubhouse. Sleeping on the deck out under the moon and stars was a little scary at first, but we soon preferred it to the close sleeping quarters below.

By 9 p.m., all of the Pirates had loaded their stuff into the Clubhouse and it was dark. We were allowed to play some hide-n-seek for about an hour before our parents told us to get in the Clubhouse and get ready for bed. We acted very cooperative and obedient knowing that they had us under their 'parent-microscopes.' We had to be very careful. As we went into the Clubhouse, Joey gave us the sign to whisper the rest of the night. I was sure that we were driving Mom and Dad crazy.

"We need to be careful tonight guys, if we screw up, the Pirates are history," Joey whispered in a hoarse voice, "Let's just act cool, eat our snacks and hang out reading comics until Mom and Dad go to bed. Then I have some plans that will be more amazing than anything we've ever done."

"What Joey? Are we going to have more fun than last summer?"

"Sssssh, keep it down Dave, I'll tell you later."

Our Clubhouse didn't have electricity, so we all turned on our Boy Scout flashlights and started trading comic books to read. I traded Dave some of my D.C. *Superman* comics for some of his *Batman Detective Comics*, but I was going to read my brand new *The Amazing Spider-Man* Marvel comic book first. It was number three and it was about Doctor Octopus. I had never read a Spiderman before. Charlie wanted to read his own Sergeant Rock comics and Joey had bought a new comic about President Kennedy's PT 109. We all wanted to see the PT 109 movie too. Johnny was eating Old Vienna potato chips and listening to our favorite DJ Johnny Rabbitt play Jan and Dean's "Surf City" on

KXOK. He was listening with his red Magnavox transistor radio. It only had one earplug, but we could still hear it while he read a *Fantastic Four* comic about Johnny Torch, his idol.

By midnight, Charlie and Johnny had fallen asleep, so we turned off their flashlights and Johnny's radio. Only Dave, Joey and me were awake. Joey whispered, "Turn out your flashlights guys, and Mickey you sneak up on the lookout and see if you see Mom or Dad. Be careful they don't see you."

"Roger," I whispered thinking that I was born for this type of skullduggery. Silently, I climbed onto the deck, keeping my head low. I had goose bumps all over as the adrenalin coursed through my body. My sweat cooled on my skin in the night air, and it made me have to pee—real bad. As I spied on my parents, I looked up at the stars. It was a beautifully clear night, and it seemed extra dark. Then it dawned on me, Joey had planned the campout on a night, when there was no moon. I felt lucky to have a brother that was so smart; he read books that he didn't have to read for school. Joey read because he wanted to learn not because he had to learn.

Silently, I surveyed our yard and the houses around the Clubhouse. All of the lights in the surrounding houses were turned off. I was scared that we were going to get caught tonight so I tried to be patient and look everywhere that somebody might see us.

After what seemed like all night, I was ready to report to Joey that the coast was clear and that I hadn't seen anybody. Then a flash caught my eye. I saw the dim glow of a red cigarette ash coming from a screened bedroom window—I figured Dad was awake and waiting to catch us sneaking out.

As quietly as I could, I slithered back into the Clubhouse and whispered, "Dad's awake and I have to pee really bad." Like a flash, I jumped out of the back window, found a bush, and peed. I was careful not to pee too close to the Clubhouse and not to step in it afterwards.

When I climbed back inside, Joey whispered directly into Dave's and my ear very quietly, "Play along with me when I talk to you guys," and then he winked.

"Let's get to sleep you guys. Good night Dave, Good night Mickey."

"Good night Joey, night Dave."

"Good night you guys."

With that, we turned off all of the flashlights, and Joey whispered to us to take a nap. Silently, Joey snuck up on the lookout deck. Dave and I were asleep before we closed our eyes.

Up on the lookout, Joey was hidden behind the rail. He had the bedroom window under surveillance. He was determined to outlast Dad, who had just lit another cigarette. It was a long night, but Joey won.

When Joey shook us, I could hardly move I was so tired.

"What time is it, Joey?"

"Sssssshhhh, it's 2, don't talk, just go out the back window and find Johnny. I'm going to wake Dave and Charlie." Quietly and careful to avoid the bush where I peed, I found Johnny sitting under an Elm tree. Our neighborhood was eerie at night in the dark, when all of the neighbors were asleep. I could faintly hear somebody's dog barking in the distance.

Joey and Dave followed me out of the clubhouse, "Where's Charlie?"

"He doesn't want to go."

"Is he scared we're going to get caught?"

"I guess so. Let's go!" and then Joey waved for us to follow him.

"Where are we going Joey?" asked Johnny.

"I got a taste for some ice cream. How about you guys?"

"Sure, I'm always hungry," said Johnny, who was the biggest and strongest of us. He was in Joey's class, and had been faster than me until this past year.

Joey started trotting, and we followed him through our neighbors' backyards. We had to jump fences about every 40 feet. We jumped these fences so often, we learned to put our hand on a post or the top fence rail, and just roll over the fence with ease. Johnny could hurdle most of the fences; he was so much taller than the rest of us. We ran through these yards so often, we were a team of one smooth, continuous action.

We knew the neighborhood backyards like our own. We knew which yards had wooden and which had wire fences, and how high each fence was. We avoided all of the yards with clotheslines, dogs, flowerbeds, and crabby people who complained to our parents. We knew, which yards had gardens with tomatoes, apples or peaches, and who kept their garden hoses in the shade if we needed a drink of cool water, when we were outside playing.

When we came to the first street that we had to cross, Joey stopped, and reminded us to get behind a bush and lay flat on the ground, if we saw any car headlights. Most importantly, he told us not to get caught no matter what and to backtrack to the Clubhouse through the backyards, not along the street, if we were spotted by somebody.

"Don't lead the cops or anybody else back to the Clubhouse you guys," he ordered.

Like a bolt, it struck Johnny, "You're taking us to the Mister Softee trucks, ain't you?"

Joey gave this really big conspiratorial smile that we could see from the dim glow of a distant street light. We all smiled back.

"How did you guess, Johnny?"

"It's the only place there's any ice cream at this time of night," he said, and we all laughed, a little too loud.

"Ssshhhh, follow me Pirates," said Joey as we trotted towards Mr. McCullough's house where two Mister Softee ice cream trucks were parked every night in his driveway during the summer.

We never saw anybody or any headlights as we ran down several streets keeping close to the shrubbery in front of the houses and away from the streetlights. At last, we saw the two Mister Softee trucks.

Silently and cautiously, we crept up to Mr. McCullough's trucks. The generators that kept the trucks' freezers working, when the trucks weren't being driven, were humming pretty loudly. Each truck had a black electric extension cord running into the McCullough's basement window to supply electricity to the generators. All we had to do was figure out how to get into the locked Mister Softee trucks.

Joey had brought a flashlight and was looking around and inside the trucks, when he came up with a plan. "Let's push open the serving window on the side of the truck and crawl in, maybe it's unlocked."

"Okay," I whispered, as I raced over and touched the aluminum metal trim around the window. My touch sent an electrical shock coursing through my body that made my hair stand on end.

"Eeeyyyoowww!" I screamed.

"Shut up, Mickey," whispered Joey, "Somebody is going to hear you."

"Ssshhocked, I got ssshhocked, don't touch the window," I stammered.

"Jeez, why don't you try the other truck Mickey?"

"I ain't touching the other of nothing. Why don't you touch it smart guy."

Everybody was laughing at me, but nobody looked very interested in touching the trucks.

"Let's lift Dave up and stick him through the window, Joey," said Johnny.

"Good idea," said Joey as he opened the window with a stick.

"You're not going to put me through a window that'll shock me."

"I'll go," I said.

"You're too big Mickey."

"Come on Dave, we won' let you touch anything.'"

"You better not Johnny or I'll scream," and then Dave laid flat and stiff on the ground.

With that, Johnny grabbed Dave's head and shoulders, Joey his waist, and I lifted his feet, then we pushed Dave through the window like a log—feet first without letting him touch any part of the window. Once inside the truck, Dave grabbed a Mister Softee hat and whispered, "Can I help you?" We all laughed quietly.

First, Dave started passing some ice cream sandwiches out the window that were in the freezer. Then Dave served us sodas without any ice. I gorged myself on a chocolate sandwich and then on a chocolate and vanilla twist sandwich that I dipped into my root beer soda. Johnny and Joey each had three sandwiches and a couple of sodas. I don't know what Dave ate and drank because I couldn't see inside the truck—it was too dark.

Everything tasted great, but we were afraid that we would be seen or heard standing between the Mister Softee trucks so we ate as fast as we could which caused me to belch real loud.

"BURPPP!" Joey and Johnny shot me stern looks just like Sister Henry that said don't be so loud, but you could tell they were laughing hard inside.

It was time to leave. Johnny grabbed Dave by his head and shoulders and started pulling him through the window, passing Dave's head and shoulders to Joey, and then Joey passed them to me as Johnny pulled Dave's feet off the floor and out of the window. Luckily none of Dave's body parts touched any part of the aluminum window frame. Joey closed the window with a small stick.

His plan had gone flawlessly, so far, so we started heading back to the Clubhouse, the same way we had come. Suddenly, Joey veered off the street and headed to a strip of woods, where we sometimes played. The woods were between two streets. Once we got to a clearing, we figured it was safe to talk normally. It was around three in the morning.

Johnny said, "Great belch!" with a loud laugh.

"I'm sorry, it just came out. I couldn't stop it."

"That's okay, it was time to get out of there anyway," said Joey.

"Were we stealing or playing Joey? Would the cops have put us in jail, if we'd been caught?"

"We didn't steal anything. We didn't have any guns, did we? We just borrowed some sandwiches and sodas that's all," said Dave.

"Yeah, Mickey, don't get your bowels in an uproar. We were doing them a favor that ice cream would have gotten spoiled. Dave you looked really scared going in that window," razzed Johnny.

"Did not."

"Did too, I thought you'd wet your pants, you looked so scared," joked Johnny as he fell and rolled around on the ground looking up at the dark sky. We were all exhausted and exhilarated by our late night adventure. As we lay on the ground, we laughed at stuff that wasn't even funny and we yawned until our eyes watered. After goofing off for a while longer, we headed back to the Clubhouse. As we crept to the edge of the woods,

Dave and I spotted some shadows as they strutted across the street and headed in our direction.

Scared and breathless, we all ran silently back into the woods until we found some places to hide. We had split up so that Joey and me hid together and Dave and Johnny hid very close to the clearing in some weeds.

"Who's that?" I whispered.

"Sshhh, don't say a word," whispered Joey as he put his finger over his lips.

A moment later two grown men strolled into our clearing, within a few of yards from where we were laying. Luckily for us, there were no streetlights, and it was so dark that no one could see very well. The men were dressed in dark clothes. One of them wore a baseball cap, and I think the other had a beard. They stunk bad like skunks. It smelled like they hadn't showered for a month. They were walking, but they were rolling a bike between them. The guy wearing a baseball cap held the bike by its handlebars.

The man with the cap said, "Did you hear something, Jake?"

"Nope, you're just a chicken turd, that's all."

"No I'm not, you're deaf. I know I heard something, Red."

"You're just scared that's all."

"I ain't. I just don't want to get caught stealing this here bike that's all. I know I heard something."

"We're not going to get caught, nobody saw us. Everybody is asleep. We haven't been caught yet, have we?"

"No I ain't and I don't want to get caught neither."

"Ain't this a nice bike? I'll bet we get ten dollars for it."

"Well let's get going so we don't get seen by the cops."

I sighed to myself, when those two men passed us and kept walking. My stomach was real full and it was starting to gurgle. I was afraid I would fart or belch any moment and then they would catch us. Once they left the clearing, we shot out of our hiding spots and ran as fast as we could in the opposite direction. None of us said another word until we climbed back into the Clubhouse completely exhausted and winded. Thankfully, we didn't run into any cops or anybody else, and we made it back without getting caught.

"Who were those guys? Where did they steal that bike? Did you recognize it?"

"It looked like a Schwinn, but I couldn't tell what color it was?"

"It ain't mine, it's in my yard. They're lucky they're gone or I would've had to whoop them," Johnny laughed.

"I've never seen those guys before," said Joey, "and they're really weird. We'd better start locking our bikes at night so they don't steal them."

As I sat there in the dark, I started thinking about what we had done and how lucky we were. If the cops had caught us sneaking around or eating Mister Softee, we would have been dead meat. And those strange men were scary wandering around at night? After thinking about it, I told Dave that I didn't want to sleep on the overlook. He didn't either.

The next morning Dad woke us up at 8:00 in the morning, fed us breakfast and had us cutting the grass and washing the car by 8:30. We didn't complain but we wondered if he knew that we had snuck out.

About ten that morning Johnny came running up to our house and told us that his dad had called the cops because his bike was stolen. Luckily, Johnny didn't tell anybody that we had seen those guys the night before because he didn't want the Pirates to get caught. We were stuck. It was good that we knew who had stolen Johnny's bike, but it was bad that we couldn't tell anybody.

Chapter 8

Journey to the Center
Of St. Ann

The last thing we wanted was to get caught by our parents hanging out where we weren't supposed to be. So, to hang out where we weren't supposed to be, we had to stay hidden and always have somebody as our lookout. The youngest guys were usually the lookouts. The Rexall Drugstore had been one of our regular hangouts ever since we were old enough to earn money to buy an ice cream cone, penny candy, candy bar, or fountain soda. We never had enough money for a banana split.

My money was kept in an empty red Folgers coffee can under my bed. I would do just about any job to make money, and we had to work because Dad didn't give us any spending money. We hunted soda bottles for their two-cent deposit, ran errands for neighbors to the Post Office or the Kroger's store, cut grass and shoveled snow for our neighbors. At our house, we cut the grass and shoveled the snow for free. Through my own enterprise, I usually had enough change in my pocket for a treat and some nickel pinball at the St. Ann Bowling Alley, which was another of our hangouts and it was close to Rexall. The problem with the bowling alley is that it smelled like cigarette smoke and stale beer.

Today, I didn't have any time or money to hang out, but we did have a whopper of an adventure planned and the guys and I had told a whopper of a lie to go on it. Jules Verne inspired our adventure when Joey read "Journey to the Center of the Earth".

We told our moms that we were taking a hike along Cold Water Creek, which was partly true. None of us told our moms that we planned to explore a huge storm sewer that was taller than any of us. We found the sewer in the middle of the St. Ann golf course when we were walking along Cold Water Creek. The sewer had a small stream of storm water running through it that poured out into the creek.

The sewer looked scary and that's what made the adventure seem so exciting. We didn't know anybody who had ever explored it before, and Joey said he thought it ran underground all the way to the center of St. Ann. We packed our lunches because we planned to be gone all day.

Saying we planned the trip is an exaggeration. All we really did was say we were going to do it. We brought something to eat, but only Greg brought one candle but he forgot to bring matches. All of us forgot our Boy Scout flashlights. Luckily, Rexall had all of our answers—they had candles and gave free matches to their customers. All we needed was money.

Joey collected everybody's money and gave it to Greg, who had already eaten his lunch. He told Greg to buy as many candles as he could, and then snatch some free books of matches when the cashier wasn't looking. Greg was chosen to buy the candles because he complained so loudly about having to "filch" some candles. He was the only one of us to bring a candle. The rest of us had to snaffle a candle or two from Rexall without getting caught. We figured if each guy swiped at least one candle, and we burned one candle at a time, we would have enough light to get us to the end of our journey, wherever that was.

The whole idea of stealing candles and walking in dark sewers shrouded in spider webs seemed pretty frightening to me, but I wasn't going to 'chicken out' in front of all of the other guys. If I got chicken, all of the guys would tease me forever, but getting teased was better than being bullied.

Gary was a greaser and a hood, which automatically qualified him as a bully. His family ran the newspaper stand on the busiest corner in the city at Ashby Road and St. Charles Rock Road. His family sold both the *St. Louis Globe-Democrat* morning edition and the *St. Louis Post-Dispatch* evening edition seven days of the week including holidays. This meant someone from his family was at the newsstand everyday from before sunrise until late at night. His family sold newspapers in the cold, in the snow, in the rain, in the sleet, and under the bright light of the sun during the hottest summer days, just like today. I felt sorry for his family.

Gary was skinny and wiry and at least eight years older than me. He wore well-worn, tight, blue jeans, black high-top tennis shoes and a white t-shirt with his *Lucky Strike* LS/MFT cigarettes rolled up into his left sleeve. Gary wasn't the only tough kid in his family; everybody was tough, even his younger sisters made me nervous.

We were hanging out and just about ready to walk into Rexall to pilfer the candles, when Gary strutted over from his newsstand and flicked his lit cigarette at me. His cigarette hit me right in the chest of my Roy Rogers t-shirt and the flying red embers flew everywhere. It scared the heck out of me.

Naturally, I screamed. Then, he growled, "What're you punks going to steal?" My soul was frozen where I stood. How did he know we were going to steal something? Was our guilt written all over our faces?

Gary stood their mocking me and laughing. My heart was racing like a bunny rabbit's when I lamely said too loudly, "I'm not going to steal anything!" As Gary walked toward us, he held out his hand and commanded, "Give me your money—PUNKS!"

Greg recoiled and obediently put his hand into his front blue jean pocket to give our money to Gary, just as 'Streak' Wilson roared up in front of Rexall on his cherry red Harley Davidson motorcycle. Time stood still, and everything was forgotten. All eyes were on Streak. Even Gary was gawking.

All of the guys knew two things—NEVER call Streak by his real name, which was Wilbur, and NEVER make fun of Streak's real name. If Streak heard you make one of those mistakes, it was rumored to result in your early death.

Actually, I wasn't really looking at Streak on his Harley today and neither were any of the other guys. We were looking at the blonde chick sitting behind him. She had her arms wrapped tightly around Streak's small waist. She wore black plastic sunglasses, white short-shorts, and the biggest smile I had ever seen. She and Streak looked like a couple of Hollywood movie stars.

Streak is one of those people you meet that is bigger than real life. He is a character in a movie. He has blonde wavy hair, stands six feet tall and ramrod straight. His muscles are always bulging out of a black sleeveless t-shirt that he wears with skintight blue jeans, wide black belt with a big silver buckle, and black motorcycle boots with silver chains across the tops. Streak oozes cool.

Everybody knows Streak. The neighbors don't like how loud he and his friends' cars and motorcycles are as they rumble and thunder up and down our streets. The cops are always on the lookout for him. All of the girls have crushes on him; and every boy in the neighborhood wants to be just like him. Streak is a legend.

The Star Community Newspaper even wrote about him when he was arrested for high-speed chases.

According to the mothers' gossip in the neighborhood, Streak had been kicked out of every elementary and high school that he attended. The only older adult that he would talk to or listen to was my dad. They seemed to have an understanding.

Streak and his buddies build fast, loud muscle cars and motorcycles and he lives right across the street from my family. I have seen his broken speedometers with their buried speedometer needles proudly displayed on his garage shelves. He's even given Joey and me a ride in one of his cars, and lets us sit on his motorcycles when Mom and Dad aren't looking.

Streak and I are buddies. Well that might be overstating the fact. He acts like he likes me, so we are at least friends.

As Streak coolly climbed off his chopped Harley cycle in front of Rexall, we all smiled and with a nod of our heads sang in unison, "How's it going Streak?" He gave us his trademark Hollywood smile in return and said, "Cool. How's it hanging boys?"

Joey knew Streak would not like Gary bullying us and taking our money. That is the strange thing about Streak. As bad as he could be, he had this certain sense of righteousness about him that caused him to do good things—sometimes.

One day, when some big kids beat Joey and me up and took our stuff, Streak found them. He beat them up, tied them into chairs and set the chairs in their driveways until their parents came home from work and untied them. They never bothered us again. You didn't want to be on Streak's bad side.

Gary was looking at Streak sheepishly and nodded hello. Suddenly, Joey got this mischievous look on his face and he said, "We're cool Streak, Gary's just giving the guys and me some money for something."

"Cool," said Streak with a smile, after seeing Joey's roguish grin, "How much is Gary giving you guys?" Then Streak took off his wire frame aviator sunglasses and looked Gary dead in the eyes.

Without cracking a smile and looking deadly serious Joey emphatically declared, *"FIVE dollars."* Now five dollars was a lot of money to us. We would have to cut and trim four yards, or shovel the snow off the driveway and sidewalks at five homes for that kind of money. It made me nervous to even to think about it.

There was a deathly silence as I gasped for air and wanted to run away. This was a showdown and it seemed like Joey had surely overplayed his hand. Then Gary said, "Yeah Streak, I told them I'd lend them five bucks. It's no problem, they're my friends."

Streak coolly smiled, looked Gary up and down, and said, "That's very cool Gary, but *GIVE* it to them, don't lend it to them. A really good friend would just give it to them, not lend it." Then Streak swaggered coolly into Rexall's air-conditioned store, while his babe sat on his 'sickle' and waited. We stood in the sweltering heat sweating like fountains.

I cringed as we circled around Joey while Gary counted out five dollars from his newspaper change and threatened to even the score under his breath. Joey looked real serious as he took Gary's money. He knew a time of reckoning would come, but until then we were all happy because we didn't have to steal any candles. In the end, we had enough money for a 15-cent ice cream cone for each of us before we left on our adventure.

Streak and Joey were our newest heroes. We gave Gary the nickname 'Chicken-Gary,' as we marched to the mouth of the storm sewer. We never tired of imitating Chicken-Gary backing down to Streak and giving Joey the five bucks. Joey was proud of his new status as we told and retold the story during our trip along the creek.

"Ol' Chicken-Gary sure looked afraid when Streak rumbled up with that good-looking chick?"

"Man, she was a fox! Did you see her legs? WOW, I thought I'd died and gone to heaven, man."

"Man, Chicken-Gary didn't say a word, when Streak told him to give us his money—man, what a gas!" said Billy as he rolled on the ground grabbing himself and laughing so hard we thought he would pee all over himself.

"I wasn't looking at her, man, I was looking at Streak's' sickle, man, that thing's cherry!" exclaimed Greg.

As Joey's brother, I felt obligated to say what everybody else was ignoring, "The only thing I was looking at was the hate in Chicken-Gary's eyes. He was madder than the devil, Joey. You better watch out, because he's going to be gunning for you now."

"Yeah, I know Mickey, but you have to admit it was a blast watching Chicken-Gary buckle to Streak's will. All he wanted to do was kick my butt, but he gave me five bucks instead because he was afraid Streak would kick his butt. It was great, man!" and then everybody laughed.

We had never explored this part of the creek because it wound through the St. Ann golf course and the employees didn't want any neighborhood kids plucking golf balls out of the creek to sell them back to the golfers. We had to sneak past Tim, the golf pro, and the groundskeepers by crawling on our bellies through the high grass along the creek's bank until we saw the gigantic yawning mouth of the storm sewer.

None of us had any idea where the storm sewer led underground. Joey reckoned it snaked around under the entire city and that we'd be able to secretly travel underground to get anywhere we wanted once we knew its routes. Today was our first such adventure and we had a couple of hours of candlelight to get us to the end—thanks to Chicken-Gary's money, Joey's guts, and Streak's cool.

As we sloshed up the creek, the mouth of the storm sewer looked like the head of a mythical dragon with a huge mouth full of teeth. The dragon's mouth was actually the round concrete sewer pipe that was bigger around than any of us were tall. It took two guys standing next to each other with their arms fully outstretched to touch both sides of the sewer's mouth at the same time. Limestone boulders were set in such a way that they looked like its eyes and teeth. The grass, weeds, trees, and shrubs looked like its scaly skin and wings.

We couldn't see much inside the sewer. It was a humongous dark hole, and we couldn't hear anything except echoes when we yelled and yodeled into its cavernous throat. Nobody said much as we sat on some of its rock teeth watching a stream of cold water drain out of its mouth and into the creek. We were quietly screwing up our courage to walk into the dragon's mouth. The adventure sounded a lot cooler before we were actually looking into the sewer ready to embark on our adventure.

The dragon's breath smelled putrid, and I had to choke down a gag. I didn't know if the sewer's smell was from somebody's toilet or just stagnant water, but I figured the worse and tried not to step into the water anymore. Whenever we saw something strange floating out of the mouth of the dragon, we would say, "Watch out for that turd, man!" In fact, we didn't know what they were, but they looked real suspicious. They could have been dragon guts for all I knew.

Our parents had always told us not to crawl into the sewers that were under our neighborhood's streets. When our various balls rolled into the sewers, we were supposed to call our parents to get them out, but those sewers were so small that you could barely crawl into them. This sewer was gigantic and we were marching in as bold as knights.

I imagined all kinds of things both alive and dead, like spiders, wild rats, rabid dogs, hissing cats, and crazy people hiding inside the dragon's bowels waiting to get us. Really, it was more like a cave than a sewer—and I shuddered when Joey gave the order, "Let's march men!" Before I knew it, Joey was leading us down the dragon's throat.

Everybody followed—Billy was second, Greg was third and I was last. I figured that I should be last since I might have to run for help if something happened to us. Since I was the fastest, I usually wanted to be first, but walking into a strange, smelly, cold, wet, dark sewer was different. It didn't seem very smart to be first, if trouble struck. Besides, I was the youngest. I didn't tell the other guys, but this sewer scared me and I was beginning to think there were better ways to spend the day than exploring it.

It was a beautiful sunny, summer day and there were any number of ways to spend it. I could play ball or capture the flag, fish for crawdads in the creek, hangout with some other guys, or just read new comics in an air-conditioned store—all of them seemed like better options to me right now, but the older guys seemed intent on exploring the sewer and I didn't want anybody calling me "Chicken-Mickey."

Walking isn't easy in a sewer. Quickly, I realized that the only thing that runs in a sewer is the water that runs on the bottom right down the center of it. So unless I wanted to slog through the running water or run in case of a real emergency, I had to straddle the running water and lumber along stiff legged and shifting my weight from side to side, which set up a kind of rolling motion. Fortunately, the beginning of the round sewer was so cavernous that it had small rock islands and tree limbs lying in the water that I could step on when my legs got tired.

As we shuffled along into the dark sewer, the large disk of bright sunlight behind us got smaller and smaller until it faded into complete darkness. That's when I realized how dark this sewer was. A cold chill made me shiver. It was so dark I couldn't see my own hand or Greg's butt, which was right in front of me. More than once, I heard somebody mumble, "dang turds" as they accidentally stepped into the water.

"Nobody's ever explored this sewer before. We're probably the first explorers to see it," exclaimed Billy proudly "I'll bet we find arrowheads and bones and other really cool stuff."

"That's impossible. No Indians were around when they built this sewer!" said Greg.

My eyes never adjusted to the dark like they did at nighttime or when we were hiding in our secret closet. It was pitch-black and I couldn't see my own hands that I was waving right in front of my face.

When Joey finally struck a match, I realized my big mistake. Being the last guy in line seemed like a good idea at first, but the last guy was the furthest from the candlelight and that was a bad idea. Any mad man or wild animal could sneak up on us and I would be the first guy killed, bitten or captured.

When Joey lit our first candle, my eyes quickly adjusted to its tiny speck of light and I immediately yelled for Joey to pass me a lit candle.

"You don't need a candle Mickey. That would be a waste of Chicken-Gary's good money," laughed Joey and the other guys. "We have a long way to go and we're going to need every candle we have or we might get lost in the dark."

At the mention of Chicken-Gary's money, Billy mumbled, "That yellow turd," and we kept trudging through the smelly sewer. Every once in a while someone would misstep and his foot would land in the water and he would curse. My Keds were already soaked, and I was starting to get hungry. I was sorry we had all eaten our lunches before we got into the sewer.

We had been trudging along for what seemed about an hour. I was bored and thinking about something else when everybody in front of me suddenly stopped. Not being able to see anything, my head ran right into Greg's butt. He snapped, "Watch out you little turd. Next time I'm going to fart on you."

"Don't fart Greg you'll blow us up with this lit candle," cackled Billy and everybody laughed except me because I was worrying about exploding farts and my position behind Greg's butt.

Having time and the opportunity to feel sorry for myself, I started thinking about the fact that I was the youngest guy in our group by two years. I deserved special considerations for being the last guy in line. This sewer was the perfect home for spiders, snakes, rats and crazy nuts waiting to kill us. I know that I was not the first guy in line, but I didn't see anybody fighting to be the last guy in line either.

It seemed to me that a person's perspective on the world depends on his position in life. The way I saw it, I was the leader in the back of our group and I deserved a lit candle because of my responsibilities as the backward leader.

So I made my plea once again, "Joey, I'm the leader back here, I need some light in case I hear something. Pass me a candle—*please!*"

Then Joey said the best thing I had heard since we started exploring the sewer, "Okay, okay. Here Billy, pass these back to Mickey."

I smiled to myself knowing that a candle and book of matches would go a long way to make me feel safer. Then I heard Billy mumble, "Here Greg, pass these back to Suzie."

Well, "Suzie" had become a fighting word, ever since 'Suzie's Tomatoes' had become my baseball team's new sponsor.

"What did you call me Billy?"

"I called you Mickey, didn't I?" he snickered.

"No, no you didn't, you called me Suzie, Billy. I clearly heard you say Suzie. Say it again and I'm going to come up there and make you sorry, if you say it one more time.'"

"Hold your horses. I'm just blowing smoke up your skirt Suzie, I mean, Mickey," he howled, "I'm sorry."

"That's it, you're dead Billy!" I said as I tried to push past Greg. Lucky for Billy, the sewer had gotten much more narrow, and Greg wouldn't budge and I couldn't push past his big butt.

"Whoa Suzie, cool down, your scaring me," Billy razzed, "You know I can't defend myself—because I don't hit girls."

With that last insult, I was grunting to push past Greg's butt and attack Billy, but Greg's butt didn't budge, and I was stuck.

I was trying to force myself to cool down when Greg said, "Here Mickey." The thought of the candle that Joey was passing to me cheered me up. As I went to grab it from Greg, I realized it wasn't a candle. They had passed me a book of doggone matches—what an insult. I didn't want to say anything because they would say I was chicken and then Billy would start calling me Suzie again, so I just said, "Thanks."

"No problem Mickey," said Joey. I thought I heard the guys chuckling, but I ignored them and we shuffled along for what seemed like another couple of hours.

So we wouldn't get lost, Joey kept us in the biggest sewer pipes when we came to junctions. About an hour earlier, Joey had explained our predicament. We had burned ten of our 18 candles. So, we knew that if we tried to backtrack we wouldn't have any candlelight for some of the way so we might get lost. Our best chance of finding a lighted opening was if we kept marching in the same direction that we were going. There had to be some kind of light or exit somewhere soon.

It had been so long since we had seen daylight that we were all beginning to feel anxious, which made everybody a little cranky. Now that we were down to our last two candles, and I didn't have any matches left, I was feeling desperate.

The further we went the more we had to crawl because the sewer pipe had gotten smaller and the mounds of debris had gotten larger in some places. We had come to several large intersections of lots of sewer pipe that were full of standing water. At those crossroads, we had to move pieces of wood and trees that had washed into the sewers and build gangplanks across the pools of water. We didn't know how deep the pools were, but we would have gotten soaked trying to wade through them. Besides, who knew what was in the water. There could have been dead bodies floating in the sewer for all we knew.

Surprisingly, we didn't run into anything alive except spiders, lots and lots of spiders and bugs. The sewer pipe that was shorter than us was uncomfortable because we had to kind of walk, crawl, and slither on our bellies at the same time. I had given up trying to walk on the sides of the sewer pipe a long time ago. The pipe was too short and my legs were too tired. My Keds were soaked, my jeans were dirty and I smelled like creek mud. I just hoped that it wasn't poop from somebody's toilet, but Joey explained we were in a storm sewer not raw sewage. I wasn't so sure because it smelled so bad.

Everybody's spirits were pretty low as Joey lit our last candle with our last match. After a few minutes of crawling he yelled, "Hey! I see some light ahead, keep moving you guys!"

As dirty and exhausted as I was, I was excited by our new prospects, so I pushed past Greg and gave an extra hard push to Billy so that I was right behind Joey.

"Hey Missy, say excuse me," Billy laughed.

"Aww let up Billy, will you?" I said as I tried to kick him.

Immediately, I realized that I should have been behind Joey the whole trip. One candle's flame provided a lot more light in the front of the line than it did in the back. I had been crawling in total darkness the whole time because I could not see past Greg. Now, as I peered around Joey's silhouette, everything seemed lighter. As I looked ahead into the sewer, I was pretty sure I saw a shaft of dim light ahead too, but it was so faint, I wondered if it was just a mirage.

As I looked more closely, I shouted, "I see the light too guys! Hurry!" And with that I pushed past Joey. I wanted to be the first guy to reach the light because we hadn't seen any real sunlight all day. I felt afraid that somehow, if I didn't hurry, the light would disappear. Until this trip in the sewer, I never wondered if the sun was going to rise. I always expected to see it every morning, but today I gained a whole new appreciation for sunlight.

The faster I crawled the brighter the pillar of light became. Being smaller than the other guys, I was able to crawl in the sewer a lot faster than them and before I knew it, I was basking in the shaft of light. The sewer pipe had gotten much taller again under the light because there was a silo made from bricks that went straight up to the source of light.

As I bathed in the light from above, I realized how wet my clothes were and how cold they felt. The sunlight was coming through a small hole above and it was so bright that I had to close my eyes when I looked up. When I shaded my eyes, all I could see was the outlines of what looked like bars. As the guys caught up with me, Billy asked, "Where in Hell are we Joey?"

"I don't know. I haven't ever been here either. Looks like we might be able to get out though."

As we looked up, there was total silence at our predicament. The fun was over. We were tired, wet, hungry, and out of matches and candles. The manhole looked way too high to reach the top. There was not a ladder or anything to grab so that we could climb out. Our rescue was so close we could see it, and yet it was so far away that we couldn't reach it. We were caught in a hellish nightmare. I was sure Chicken-Gary would be laughing at us now.

With none of us talking to the other, I realized how loud the noise above us was. It sounded like traffic.

"Do you guys hear traffic? Which street do you think it is?"

"Maybe the Rock Road," said Joey.

"We have to be farther than that. We've been walking all day, man. I'm tired."

"I don't know what direction we headed once we got in the sewers. Do you know?"

"No, I don't know where we are, man."

"What're we going to do Joey?" I pleaded.

"Let's boost one of us up there and see if we can get out of here."

Boosting one of us up wasn't going to be easy. We guessed there was an iron manhole cover with a hole above us that was easily higher than ten feet. Billy was the tallest and strongest, Greg and Joey were about the same height, but Greg was heavier and I was the shortest and the lightest. My speed wasn't any help. At that moment, I was wishing I had super powers that would let me grow tall or stretch like the *Metal Men* in D.C Comics.

"If I was a super hero, I'd be out of here in a flash," I said.

"That's a great idea, Mickey," said Billy, "We'll be the Fantastic Four. Joey, you're Dr. Richard Reed, Greg you're Benn Grim, I'll be Johnny Storm, and Mickey you're Suzie Storm," and then he belly laughed so hard I hoped he'd get the hiccups.

"Shut up Billy, you're not so funny! I was thinking of the Metal Men anyway, you Tin-head," I said in my most offending way. The Suzie jokes were definitely getting to me and so was Billy. I was going to be glad to be away from him once we were out.

Joey, Greg, and Billy tried a couple of different ideas to build a pyramid high enough so that one of them could reach the manhole. None of them worked. Finally, they decided that they needed my help to get high enough to reach the manhole cover.

We started our pyramid, with Joey and Greg's backs close to the brick wall so that they could lean up against it for support, as the pyramid got higher. First, they bent over and put their hands on their knees. Next, Billy climbed on top of their backs, and stood with one of his muddy tennis shoes on each of their backs. They complained loudly about their shirts getting really wet, dirty, and smelly from Billy's shoes. Finally, I climbed up and over Joey and Greg trying to be careful not to hurt them so that I could stand on Billy's shoulders and shinny out the manhole.

The best part of my job was that I got to put my muddy feet all over Billy as I climbed out over him. It felt really great to grind both of my muddy wet heels into his feet, knees, arm, back, neck, and finally his head, while I listened to him moan. "Ooooww, watch it twerp, hey that hurt, you're doing this on purpose Mickey, Oooouch!"

At the very end, I gave Billy an extra little grind on his shoulder and stomped him on the top of his head, as I tried to push open the iron manhole using my shoulders and back because it was so heavy. Sarcastically I said, "Aren't you glad I'm not wearing my high heels, Billy?" The manhole was so heavy I couldn't push it open and crawl out. All I could do was put my mouth to the little hole and yell at the top of my voice and hope that someone could hear me.

Down in the sewer we had all hoped and prayed that we would find a ladder. The problem was, we found the firefighter too. Unbeknownst to us, the manhole was right next to the fire station. Unluckily or luckily, depending on your perspective, a firefighter heard me. He grabbed his crowbar, a ladder, and his crew and they rescued us, which was good and bad.

It was good that we got out, but it was bad that we got caught. The firefighters said that what we had done was very dangerous, and instructed us about gases that collect in sewers, which could explode. Naturally, they lectured us about how we were very lucky that we didn't get lost, hurt, or killed. Next, they took us home in the fire truck, which caused quite a stir in the neighborhood.

Our moms insisted that we go back to the fire station with the nice firefighters and wash out their truck and our clothes that smelled and looked real nasty. We also got a lecture from our mothers about how we could've been killed. None of us really listened about the dying part of the lecture, the trip seemed scary, but it didn't seem "that" dangerous. Parents always worry too much. We know how to take care of ourselves.

Mom grounded us for a couple of days and had us wash all of the floors in the house, even the wall-to-wall carpet in the living room. After washing every floor in the house, we had to wax the linoleum tile and hard wood floors. Mom's thoughts about clean floors and soulful absolution were intertwined and they both required kneeling on hard floors.

Mom insisted that our souls and her floors were never properly cleansed unless we cleaned them while on our hands and knees. She rejected the modern concept that mops or other conveniences were adequate to the task of washing away the dirt on her floors or the dirt in our souls. She preferred that we wash her floors holding a bristle scrub brush while kneeling next to a bucket of sudsy Spic-n-Span. After being thoroughly scrubbed with soap, she insisted that her floors be rinsed with a series of clean cloths and buckets full of fresh water. The last stage of absolution for her floors and our souls was applying a thick coat of Bruce Floor wax for protection from future transgressions.

After two days of kneeling on hard floors, Joey's and my knees were very sore and blistered. I could hardly crouch to be the catcher for our ball game against the Astronauts.

There is never anything worse than getting caught hanging out where you aren't supposed to be.

Chapter 9

B.S.

I didn't really want to visit our cousins who lived in the country, but Grandma told me I needed to try new things to become well rounded. So, we were driving to Indiana to visit the Carmichael Clan the morning after my 'under the lights' baseball game, which Grandma got to see. We had beaten the Comets 12 to one, and it was the best game we had played all summer. Coach Starr had given us a pep talk after our last practice, and told us to be proud of our uniforms. He said it was time to quit whining and quit letting the other teams tease us about our team's sponsor. He told us that if we called each other 'Suzie' or 'Tomato' whenever one of us made a good play the other teams couldn't razz us anymore. He said if we called each other Suzie, it wouldn't hurt our feelings anymore. His advice worked.

Whenever I threw out a Comet player trying to steal a base, the guys yelled, "That's the way to throw the tomato, Suzie!" We all laughed. It was fun. I started wearing my new red ball cap wherever I went, and if somebody asked me what the 'S' stood for, I'd say Suzie, and chuckle. They'd look at me weirdly.

Grandma affectionately called our Carmichael cousins Hoosiers, which made me wonder how a Hoosier acted and what they ate. Our cousins lived in southern Indiana near Vincennes. The best part of the trip was that Grandma came with us. Mom drove the Ol' Gray Mare because Dad said we needed to use third gear. We were visiting all of the relatives Grandma grew up with before she moved to St. Louis to study nursing. Dad stayed at home because he had to work.

Although I was unsure about the trip, I'd go anywhere and do anything to spend time with Grandma. Mom secretly told us Grandma was a little nervous that we wouldn't like our country cousins because they were different. The Carmichaels lived in the country and the relatives that we were staying with didn't have any kids. They were older than Grandma. Being born in St. Louis city, and raised in its north county suburbs, I had never lived in the country, but Joey and I had camped with the Boy Scouts. I just hoped that our cousins had horses, preferably wild. I wanted to ride a horse just like the Lone Ranger's horse, Silver.

Our trip took most of the day, because we never drove faster than 45 miles per hour, and we stopped for gas every chance we got. Mom and Grandma were always afraid we'd run out of gas. For lunch, we stopped at a roadside rest stop that had a picnic table. We ate ham sandwiches, Old Vienna potato chips, Grandma's famous blonde brownies filled with chocolate chips, and we drank an entire aluminum thermos filled with ice-cold lemonade. We stopped for potty breaks every half-hour after lunch.

The Ol' Gray Mare didn't have air-conditioning, so in the hot afternoon sun, all of the car's windows and vents were wide open. That way, the hot wind could blow through the car and dry our sweat. In between spotting and counting license plates from different states, and playing card games, Joey and I fought and argued about who had crossed over the other's imaginary boundary line on the seat. While Joey read some library book, I read comics. I didn't intend to read any library books during my summer vacation. I had bought a new *Amazing Spider-Man* at the last gas station that I was reading. This time Spider-Man was fighting a Lizard man. I really liked Spider-Man because he was a kid just like me.

We were going to stay at our great-Uncle Willard and great-Aunt Blanche's cottage styled home. Aunt Blanche was the sister of my great-grandmother Gigi, and when I first saw her I went whomper-jawed. She looked exactly like Gigi, whom I loved dearly. I couldn't take my eyes off of her. And when I hugged her, she even giggled like Gigi, so I hugged her a lot. Their home had lots of large oak shade trees standing sentinel around it. It was as cool as a cave inside their cottage styled home and on their porch even on a blistering hot summer day. They had lived in the same house for 50 years, and their love for their home showed everywhere I looked.

I was disappointed to find out our Hoosier cousins weren't farmers, and that they didn't even have a white horse named Silver. The good news was they were surrounded by farms and lived next to a dairy farm. Aunt Blanche had the most fantabulous garden I had ever seen. They could grow anything a person could eat. Uncle Willard was a court bailiff and a diehard Cardinals baseball fan. Joey and I loved it when he acted like an umpire, when we played 'pitch and catch.' Uncle Willard would stand behind me and call balls and strikes, while using the names of ball players just like Jack Buck and Harry Caray did on the radio.

Uncle Willard said things like, "It's the bottom of the ninth of the seventh game of the World Series and Yogi Berra steps to the plate with two outs for the Yankees. Berra's batting .289 and he's about to face Joey McBride, the best pitcher the *St. Louis Cardinals* have. Joey gets his signal from his brother, Mickey, who is the Cardinals' best catcher ever. Here's Joey's windup and the pitch. It's a low fastball, *Steerike THREE*! Yogi Berra goes down swinging for the third time today. The Cardinals win the World Series!!!" Uncle Willard made it sound so exciting that it felt just like we were actually playing for the Cardinals in the World Series.

Aunt Blanche's cooking was every bit as good as Uncle Willard's game calling. She lovingly prepared the best food I had ever eaten, and that's what she did the whole time we were there—cook and bake. Everything she served was homemade and usually homegrown, even their milk, butter and cheese came from the dairy next door. She said she loved to cook for me as much as I loved to eat her cooking.

After I would eat something she made, I'd say, "I have never eaten anything this good Aunt Blanche. What do you call it?"

She'd laugh, tell me what it was and say, "Mickey, just you wait. I'm getting ready to fix something even better. You'll love it."

My mouth would start watering just thinking about what she was going to bake, fry or mix next. It was like living in a restaurant. She never served anything modern that was pre-made or frozen in an aluminum tray. The only thing I didn't understand was why they never had kids. When I asked Grandma, she said they just weren't blessed with their own family. I guess that is why they loved having us visit. Any kid would have loved having them as parents.

We had visited for three days and had met all kinds of cousins. I was sad that we were leaving in the morning. When I asked Grandma why we were leaving she said, "Guests are like fish, after three days, they smell."

I didn't understand what she meant. I took a bath every night and Aunt Blanche smelled like sugar and flour. I loved nuzzling up next to her on the couch in the evenings to fall asleep while we listened to the radio. They didn't have a TV set.

In the mornings, I'd always wake up in a big feather bed wondering how I got there. I could've stayed with Aunt Blanche and Uncle Willard the rest of my life. They loved having us stay with them.

We visited Aunt Blanche and Uncle Willard's Baptist church for Sunday services the day before we left. Mom promised us that it wasn't a sin, so I didn't worry about missing Mass. Everyone there was very happy to see Grandma again and meet her family. I didn't know that Grandma had become a Catholic, when she married Grandpa. The church services were so long; I didn't think we'd ever get home again. When we did Aunt Blanche started cooking and the smells coming from her kitchen had my mouth watering while Joey and I played catch. Our last homemade dinner together included fried chickens that were taken and plucked from their coop, mashed potatoes and gravy, green beans with bacon and onions, biscuits bigger than baseballs, honey from their hives, and fresh churned butter. For dessert, we ate a big slice of hot apple pie that was made from scratch.

I was so full I thought I would bust wide open. I only kept eating because Aunt Blanche kept saying things like, "Sweetie, can't you finish those green beans, they're fresh," or "Come on Mickey, I know you can eat that last piece of chicken. It'll just go to waste." I didn't want to disappoint her, so I ate for all I was worth, and determined not to eat so much that I'd throw up like I did with the pancakes.

Everyone was just as full as me. All the adults could do was sit in lawn chairs under the huge shade trees holding glasses of Aunt Blanche's sweet tea. She kept her sweet tea in a big blue and white bowl that had a picture of people living on a farm in its bottom. The bowl had a matching ladle. Her tea had so much sugar in it she had to keep a piece of cheesecloth over the bowl so the flies wouldn't climb in and drink it all.

Needing one last adventure, Joey and I decided to go exploring before we left in the morning. Besides, we needed to get some exercise and wear off dinner.

It was late afternoon. We ran straight for the neighboring dairy farmer's barbed wire fence and crawled under. The last couple of days, we had strolled along with the cows in the pasture behind the dairy barn. We even watched the farmer milk his cows, when Aunt Blanche asked us to fetch a pail of milk. I was getting used to the big cows but I kept my distance and didn't bother them. They made me jittery.

During our first expedition into the dairy pasture, I learned three important lessons about cows. Cow pies aren't something you eat; you don't want to step into fresh cow pies; and you can sail dried cow pies a pretty good distance. Uncle Willard laughed the whole time I was scraping and washing the fresh cow pies out of the treads of my Keds.

As we adventured along, I closely monitored the ground for unseen cow pies lurking in the tall pasture grass. It seemed like there were as many cow pies in the pasture as stars in the summer sky. You could hardly avoid them. Today, we were hiking a different route than we had taken on our previous adventures.

We crawled under more fences, crossed a creek a couple of times, and went through a couple of stands of large oak trees. As a cool evening breeze gently started blowing, we found ourselves standing under a ginormous oak tree.

Its branches spread so far out, there had to be a mile of shade to lie under. It was so big around, together, we couldn't reach around it and touch our fingers. We even tried lying on the ground and touching our hands and feet, but it didn't help; the tree was just too big around. The tree partially shaded a crystal clear pond where we could see fish swimming through the moss near the shallow shoreline.

It would've felt great to go swimming in the water, which was ice cold. After talking it over, we decided not to because we didn't know what was in the water. Snakes? Snapping turtles? Man-eating fish? We didn't know and more importantly we didn't want to know.

We figured we had been gone a few hours, and were surprised that we hadn't seen more cows during our trip. We talked about our trip to Indiana and baseball as we laid down in the grass in the tree's shade. After lying around a while, we figured it was time to head back to Aunt Blanche's, and tried to remember the exact route we walked to get here. It was hard because the sun wasn't as bright as it had been and we weren't exactly sure which way we had traveled.

As we trudged along, Joey noticed a cow a long way off standing alone on the top of a hillside behind us.

"That's the first cow I've seen in a long time."

"Where? Oh yeah, I see it," I replied.

We didn't pay the cow much attention as we traipsed and talked our way through the pasture trying to figure the best route home. The sun was getting a lot bigger and redder as it fell through the blue cloudless sky that was getting darker.

Looking around for a landmark of some kind, Joey noticed the cow again. This time it was a little closer.

"That cow looks bigger than the others. Do you think it's lost and is following us?"

"Maybe. Remember how those cows followed us into the dairy barn?"

"Yeah, that was cool, wasn't it?

Looking ahead, we kept marching towards the setting sun because Joey was convinced Aunt Blanche's home was in the west. The sun had gotten even bigger and redder, as it started dropping behind the hill ahead of us. Looking back over my shoulder, I noticed that same cow again.

"That cow's following us for sure Joey. Look. It's right behind us now, and you're right it's a lot bigger than the others. Let's walk a little faster," I said a little worried.

"Okay Mickey. Maybe this one's not as friendly as the others. Maybe we should run some."

"Yeah, okay, maybe it's not friendly. It looks like it might be chasing us."

After putting on a little sprint, I looked back again, and became real concerned very quickly, "Run Joey! Run as fast as you can. That cow's chasing us for sure," and with that I started running full speed down the middle of the pasture ahead of Joey.

"Forget the cow pies Mickey. Run as fast as you can that cow's gaining on us for sure." And with that urge, we were both hotfooting it through the grass pasture as fast as our Keds could carry us. We were even hurdling over some of the taller grass so we didn't get slowed down.

Seeing the cow get closer, Joey yelled, "Mickey, you run to the right, I'm going to run to the left. Let's confuse it."

"Okay!" I yelled over my shoulder. I felt desperate as we split apart in the middle of the pasture. I started running straight towards the only tree I could see that was on my right. It was big and it looked like a great climbing tree. I saw Joey running towards the barbed wire fence that ran along a line of trees on the left side of the pasture.

Watching constantly over my shoulder, I saw that the cow was chasing me and not Joey. It was really building up a head of steam as it trampled over the grass and snorted loads of snot out of its nose, which had a ring in it.

Having never been around cows before this trip, I didn't know they could run so fast. When we played around the dairy barn, the cows looked like they could barely walk to the barn to be milked. This cow ran like a deer trying to win an Olympic gold medal.

Regardless of the cool evening air, this cow had me in a drenching hot sweat. My t-shirt, hair and face were soaked as sweat dripped off my nose onto my lips and chin.

Veering towards the tree, I prayed I could climb it, when I got there. As I got nearer, I carefully inspected it for a low limb to grab, or a foothold to help boost me into it—*FAST*—the cow was quickly closing the gap between us.

Tree climbing is a year-round competitive sport in St. Ann. It doesn't matter whether you are walking down a street, along the creek, or in the park. If we see a tree that looks challenging, we dare whoever we are with to climb it. The guy who challenges the other guy has to remember the one major rule, when you challenge somebody to climb a tree; you are expected to climb it first. It's the 'Manly Rule.'

The Manly Rule keeps tree climbing a fair and honest sport. You can't dare someone without daring yourself. You can't call someone "chicken" unless you climbed the tree first and they wouldn't try.

Just last week Dave and I dared each other to climb every tree on our street as high as we could. All totaled we each climbed 67 various trees. It took us two whole days. The second day we had to change from our jean shorts and t-shirts into long jeans and sweatshirts because our legs, arms, hands and faces were scraped raw and bloody from shimmying up every elm, oak, maple, and sycamore that we could find. We even climbed a prickly hawthorn and a couple of sticky sap white pines. At the end of second day, we were flat out tired, bloody and sore. Neither of us had chickened-out and I had learned a lot more about climbing trees.

Any tree climber worth his salt knows that the tallest trees aren't necessarily the hardest trees to climb. It all depends on the types of branches and bark a tree has. The best climbing branches grow low to the ground and are close together all of the way up the trunk of the tree. The best bark to shimmy up is smooth so it doesn't cut into your skin and it isn't sticky with sap. The best bark to walk on is rough so you don't slip.

Pines are a mess to climb even though their branches are low to the ground and their bark is smooth because their sap is so sticky your fingers stick together for days. You don't dare touch your hair after climbing a pine until you use turpentine to clean your hands first.

Personally, I would rather climb a sticky pine than any tree with sharp thorns any day of the week. They are the worst. A sycamore's bark is slippery and in the spring its cotton balls will choke you to death. Oaks are okay, but tricky because when they get old, their limbs are so high and far apart you need a rope. I prefer to shimmy up maple trees because they don't grow too tall, and their branches can grow low to the ground and are smooth.

The closer I got to the tree in the pasture, the more it looked like an old maple. I noticed a nice big, low hung limb straight ahead. The only question was could I reach it before the cow got to me. Just then the cow bellowed so loudly, it scared the bejeebers out of me and an extra shot of adrenaline coursed through my sweaty, tired and scared body. That shot of adrenaline actually made me leap just a little higher so that I was able to grab that thick limb that was just high enough so that the cow couldn't reach me. I was able wrap both of my arms and my legs around the limb. Holding on for dear life, I crawled on the limb towards the tree's trunk. The cow bellowed and shook its horns, which were just a foot or so below me.

Now standing in the crook of the thick limb, the cow stood directly beneath me snorting and pawing the ground. My heart was pounding so hard I could see my shirt move with each beat. The cow was really angry that it hadn't caught me. It was bellowing so loudly the leaves shook. Although I was shaky and trapped in a tree, I felt pretty safe while I wondered what had happened to Joey.

Holding onto to the tree for dear life, I craned my head toward the fence looking for Joey. I was shocked to see him sitting behind an older man wearing a straw cowboy hat and a big smile. They were both riding on the back of the biggest and whitest horse I had ever seen. As they rode up to my tree, the man waved his straw hat over his head and yelled at the cow, "Get out of here Spike," and then to me he said, "Don't fall out of that tree Mickey!"

"I won't but you better watch out for that cow."

"Shoot this ain't a cow Mickey. Spike's a bull, and all he knows how to do is brag and bully others around, but he ain't going to bully Ol' Hercules here," he said as he patted his horse's thick, muscular neck.

Looking embarrassed, the bull put his head down, and harmlessly skedaddled. It was hard to believe that Spike was the same bull that had just chased us a country mile and treed me like a cat.

With Hercules standing guard under me, the farmer laughed and said, "Don't you boys know the difference between a cow and a bull? Now jump down here in front of me so you don't fall off Mickey," he laughed.

"Yes sir," I said as I slid down out of the tree onto Hercules' back, which seemed as wide as a kitchen table. "Did you forget your saddle mister?" I snickered thinking it must have looked funny to see the three of us stacked one behind the other on Hercules muscular back, when he didn't even have a saddle.

"Shoot no, Hercules doesn't like saddles. You ain't farm boys are you?"

"No sir, we're from St. Louis."

"I expect you are son. I expect you are," he said as he laughed again. Everything he said was accompanied with a chuckle or a laugh.

"How'd you know my name, mister?"

"Your Grandma told me, when she called and asked me to look for you boys."

"Do you know my Grandma?"

"Shoot yeah," he laughed again, "Ruth and I grew up on these farms together."

"Well, what's your name mister?"

"Goldie MacDonald," he proclaimed proudly.

Then I snickered, "Does anybody call you Ol' MacDonald?"

"You wouldn't be the first, Mickey," he laughed as we slowly rocked and rode through the pasture.

"Why did the cow, I mean bull, chase us Mr. MacDonald? We weren't hurting anything."

"That's what bullies do Mickey. They chase you because they know you're scared and you're in their pasture."

162

"Is Spike your bull, Mr. MacDonald?"

"First call me Goldie like everybody else. Yeah Spike's my bull. I should've gotten rid of him a long time ago, but I'd miss him too much."

Sitting high on Hercules' muscular back, Goldie wrapped his arms around me as he held the thick leather reins in his strong hands. He made me feel real safe, and I thought about the fact that Goldie was the first older man I could remember to give me a hug. I wondered if my grandpas' hugs would've felt like this if they were alive.

As we slowly rode home through the pastures, the sunset got more and more beautiful by the moment. The bright blue sky changed from orange to pink to purple as the full moon rose over another hillside all at the same time. I heard a bird calling from the top of a nearby maple tree. When I looked closer, it was a bright red Cardinal.

"Were you and my Grandma friends?"

"Well, we still are friends Mickey. I was always trying to spark her. I even took her for her first ride in an automobile."

"Did she like driving fast, when she was a kid?"

"Yeah, Ruth loved having the wind blow through her hair, when we'd get going real good downhill. I was heart broke, when she moved to St. Louis."

"Can you tell us more stories about Grandma, Goldie?"

"Sure can," and, as we hoofed it home, Goldie told us more stories about him and Grandma growing up as farm kids in southern Indiana. His deep and gentle voice and the rocking motion of Hercules' broad shoulders made me realize how tired I was. I finally leaned back further against Goldie's chest and fell asleep listening to him talk.

When we got to Aunt Blanche's house, I woke up with all of the noise of everybody coming out to hug us and ask us what had happened. Aunt Blanche had baked a fresh blueberry cobbler to celebrate Goldie finding us, but I was so tired I didn't eat anything before Goldie walked me half-asleep to the deep feather mattress for my last night's sleep in the country.

I felt really sad during our drive home. I didn't even argue with Joey when he crossed the boundary on the seat. Halfway home we stopped and ate our delicious lunch that Aunt Blanche had fixed and packed for our trip. As I rubbed my stomach after my blueberry cobbler, I smiled thinking about how well rounded I had become on our vacation.

Chapter 10

Friends Forever

I t was impossible to understand and I didn't want to believe it, so I prayed that it wasn't true. We had all said that we would be friends forever. We did everything with each other even though we didn't see each other every day. Allen didn't go to St. Kevin. He lived in a Protestant part of the neighborhood on Ashby Road.

Allen was an apple-cheeked kid who liked flirting with girls, and the girls liked him because he was so friendly. He and Joey combed their hair alike, but Allen's older sister had bleached his hair blonde. None of us bleached our hair so Allen took a lot of kidding. He didn't care. He was an only son so he didn't have to wear hand-me-down clothes, and he was always dressed cool.

Allen was different in other ways too. He didn't play baseball or other sports; he was a talker and he told lots of jokes. He was always laughing and he was a fun guy to be around. Whenever Allen would see us walking down his street, he would tell us some great jokes that we had never heard or take us into his basement to play some records on his high fidelity stereo. Personally, I can't remember a joke, but Allen remembered every joke that ever made him laugh. His dad even kept a rolling rack of comedy records in his basement that Allen had memorized. That's how we met Allen.

One day a bunch of us were walking by his house to go to the park to play some football. Allen saw us, and came out to the sidewalk to say hello. After we met each other, he invited us into his basement to listen to some comedy records. It was a cold fall day so we accepted his invitation.

His mom made us some slices of sugar bread and hot chocolate and before the afternoon was over, we were all best friends. Lots of days we would go over to his house to hang out and listen to our favorite Jerry Lewis, Bob Hope, Peter Sellers, Jackie Gleason, and Red Skelton comedy records. He even had some Red Foxx records that his parents wouldn't let us play, but we did anyway, when they weren't home or couldn't hear us. I giggled at a lot of Red Foxx's jokes that I didn't understand because the older guys were laughing.

This summer Allen's favorite song was "Hello Mudduh, Hello Fadduh! (A Letter from Camp)." A hilarious guy named Allan Sherman, who wore black plastic glasses just like Allen, sang it.

That's why we couldn't believe the rumor. All of the time we spent with Allen was happy and fun, how could he be dead?

I was hoping it was a bad joke, when Dave came up to our house and told us that Allen had drowned. Joey and I didn't believe Dave. It didn't seem possible that one of our best friends was actually dead. I had never had a friend die before. We were kids. We were too young to die.

"How'd he drown Dave?"

"I don't know."

"Where'd he drown, Legion Pool? Couldn't he swim? I thought all of us guys could swim."

"I don't know if he could swim Joey, I just heard that he drowned in the Meramec River that's all."

"Well, I'll bet Allen's not dead. This is one of his jokes. Let's go over to his house and see," said Joey. "He'll be there laughing his head off. I know it." Off Joey went, jogging down the street, determined to see our friend. Dave and I ran to keep up.

As we got to St. Phillip Lane, we saw Billy and Greg playing catch. They hadn't heard about Allen either, so they joined us. On St. Barbara Street, we found Johnny and Larry. They joined us too. We were jogging pretty fast so we were on Ashby Road before we knew it. There were so many of us, we looked like we were going to play baseball, but Joey was in the lead and he wasn't smiling.

Nobody was laughing or joking like we usually were. All of the guys were quiet, and that is when I thought that Allen had made up a really bad joke this time. Everybody was very serious and nobody was laughing.

When we got to the front yard of Allen's house, Joey didn't hesitate. He skipped up to the front porch's steps, knocked on the front door and hollered; "Can Allen play?" before any of us were even in the yard. No one answered the door.

After a minute, Joey looked at us with a quizzical look and then knocked again a little louder, "Can Allen play?" He was determined to have Allen answer the door.

"Nobody's home, Joey. Maybe we should come back later," said Billy, as we gathered around the porch.

"Look," said Joey pointing, "His dad's car's here, they just don't hear me, everybody must be in the basement." Suddenly the front wooden door opened and there stood Mrs. Lamb behind the screen door. We all noticed she wasn't wearing her big smile like usual.

"Hi Missus Lamb. Can Allen play?" Joey asked with a quiet desperation in his voice that you could feel more than hear.

Mrs. Lamb opened the screen door and said, "I'm sorry boys, but Allen can't play today. Allen's gone boys, my Allen is gone, he drowned yesterday," and with that news we all collapsed and started bawling like babies where we stood. With tears streaming from her eyes, Mrs. Lamb stepped onto the porch and grabbed Joey hard to hug him. Joey didn't pull away. He stood there hugging Mrs. Lamb, both of them needing each other. Then we all rushed up to Mrs. Lamb so that she would hug us too, even Billy.

I don't remember ever being that sad except when my great-grandmother Gigi had died four years before. The thought of Allen's death was unimaginable to me. I couldn't bear the thought. We wouldn't ever sit in Allen's basement and play his funny records ever again. It was very hard to accept that I would never ever see Allen or Gigi ever again. They were dead. I knew I would miss Allen forever, just like Gigi.

Our parents didn't want us to go alone to Allen's visitation at the Collier Funeral Home. They wanted to come along, but we insisted that we go alone. After we all got dressed in our best Sunday church clothes, we met at the corner and walked in a procession down to Collier's along the shoulder of St. Charles Rock Road. It was a beautiful sunny day with big, white fluffy clouds, and it wasn't too awfully hot even with a tie and sport coat.

Since my parents weren't with me, I felt more grown-up, but I was pretty nervous. I had never been in a funeral home or seen a dead body before. I didn't know what to expect. My parents didn't let me go to Gigi's funeral. They thought I was too young, but I was always sad they didn't let me.

Allen had drowned when his family camped at Meramec State Park. We were told the Meramec River had really strong undertow currents, and that Allen simply went under the water and never came up again.

Our parents told us to never swim in the Meramec River, ever, even if we were with our Scout troop.

It was very hard to forget the vision of a grappling hook being used to catch Allen's body and pulling it from the river. I even had nightmares. I felt very sad and sighed very deeply about the fact that Allen was dead.

As we entered Collier's, its massive black door closed behind us shutting out the bright sunshine except the little bit of light that filtered through the heavy drapes covering the windows. The building's entrance foyer felt very cold from the air conditioning, and it took a minute for my eyes to adjust to the darkness. The air smelled like my Aunt Helen's flowery perfume, which was way too sweet and way too strong. I wondered if Allen liked it.

A grandfatherly looking man with wire frame glasses dressed in a dark suit greeted us and took us to see Allen.

I had an urge to bolt and run to a shady spot near the creek that wasn't too far away, but I gritted my teeth and stayed. I heard Billy whisper to Johnny that Allen would've liked it better if they called his room a 'saloon' instead of a salon, which was a joke on one of Red Foxx's records. Nobody laughed, not even Billy.

As we entered the salon, Allen's mom immediately came over and smiled through her red, swollen and teary eyes, "Thanks for coming boys! I'm sure Allen's happy. I know he is looking down from heaven right now and is happy to see us all together."

"You're welcome Mrs. Lamb. We want to say goodbye to Allen," said Joey very somberly.

"It's very sweet Joey and we appreciate your visit. Will you to do something for me? Well really, it's not for me, it's for Allen. Please?"

"Sure Mrs. Lamb, anything," Joey was definite.

"Will you comb Allen's hair, Joey? You and Allen comb your hair the same way. The funeral home didn't quite comb Allen's hair the way he usually combs it. Will you please comb Allen's hair for him?"

"Sure Mrs. Lamb, anything," Joey repeated without any hesitation.

All of us looked at each other shocked. The idea of touching a dead person's hair seemed pretty creepy to us. There is no way I could've done it and I didn't have any idea how Joey could do it either, but Joey felt different than the rest of us.

"Thanks Joey so much, we really appreciate it," said Mrs. Lamb as she led us over to Allen.

"It'll be easier if I have some water Mrs. Lamb," said Joey as he looked down into Allen's face and with that Allen's mom went to get some water.

I stood back from the casket looking at Allen. He was lying there without laughing, and I kept asking myself if his face looked like my friend Allen the way I remembered him. It didn't. I did recognize his blond hair, but it wasn't Allen's hairstyle. The one mystery that I couldn't figure out was why God would let a young kid like Allen die. Allen was an all-around great guy. He was everybody's friend.

When Mrs. Lamb returned, she was holding a paper Dixie cup full of water and Allen's long black comb, which he always kept in the back pocket of his pants.

Joey took Allen's comb in his right hand and held the cup of water in his left as he deftly dipped the comb into the water again and again and patiently combed each hair on Allen's head until they were all in place. Joey acted cool the whole time, and when he was done, Allen's golden hair looked just like it always did.

"It's perfect Joey," said Mrs. Lamb as she lovingly admired her son, "He looks just like an angel—thank you!"

"You're welcome Mrs. Lamb. Allen would've done the same for me," sniffled Joey. "We always said we'd be friends forever."

Chapter 11

Build a Better Rat Trap
And the World Will Beat
A Path to Your Door

D ad says he always gets his best ideas while he is working, and that's how I got the best idea I ever had—working with Bob. Bob is the only African-American person I know. He works at our Kroger store. He and I are buddies. I never see any other African-American people unless I go downtown with my family. I like working with Bob and when I visit him, I don't take any of my friends with me because Bob pays me a nickel, dime or quarter to help him.

In St. Ann, I only see people that look pretty much like me. I don't really think about them as being like me or different from me because we are all pretty much the same. We all live in similar houses, have similar size families, like the same things, and we go to the same churches. Take Tony. He is taller, thinner, and has blonde hair. His family comes from the country, talks with a country accent and is Catholic. Frank is Italian, about my height, and is Catholic too. Frank is lucky because his mom sends him to school with a meatball or steak sandwich every day.

Some of the other kids get a jelly sandwich. Mom makes me bologna, salami, or Braunschweiger, and of course, cheese sandwiches on Friday. Then there is Tommy. He is Irish. I also know Mr. Kessler, who is Jewish. He owns a clothing store next to Rexall. His clothes are pretty expensive so we don't shop there very often.

I don't really think much about any of our differences because we all live or work in the same neighborhood. Bob took the Bi-State bus up and down the St. Charles Rock Road between Kroger and his home in Wellston until he "finally broke down and bought" an orange 1954 Chevrolet Bel Air. He says he likes driving a lot more than standing in the heat, rain, and snow waiting for the bus.

Bob is the store janitor and he is always dressed in a clean, white uniform. To me, he looks like my newest St. Louis Cardinal hero Bob Gibson. They are both African-American and they are both named Bob. Naturally, I assumed they knew each other, but Bob told me he doesn't know "Mr. Gibson," but he greatly admires his pitching just like me. Bob calls everybody, Mister or Missus or Miss. He even calls me, "Mister Mickey." I never understood why. He said it's because he is from the South wherever that is. It never dawned on me to call him "Mister Bob." His nametag simply says, 'BOB' so that's what I call him.

It doesn't feel strange to me to call Bob by his first name. I call all of my best friends by their first names.

Bob and I have been friends for as long as I can remember. When I was younger, I helped him with his work while Mom shopped. As I got older and could sneak up to Kroger by myself, I would just go hang out with him.

We talk while we collect shopping carts from the parking lot, empty and clean trashcans and break down cardboard boxes to put them in the empty truck trailer that is always backed up to the loading dock in the back of the store. The trailer is hauled off every week when it is full of cardboard boxes and fruit and vegetable crates. The guys and I usually play in the Kroger trailer on Sunday afternoons when the store is closed and there is nothing else to do.

We never told our parents where we were when we were playing in the truck trailer. They would've told us "No." They would've said it was dangerous and we would get hurt or the police would arrest us and throw us in jail. Our parents had all sorts of threats and things they would say to dissuade us from doing something 'dangerous.' It was just easier not to tell them where we were going.

I was loading flattened brown cardboard boxes into the truck trailer on a hot, sunny afternoon when I was struck with the greatest idea I ever had to get back at Booger and Butch.

Booger and Butch have been bullying us for years. We were too young and small to beat them up so we needed an idea to get back at them without getting beat up by them—again.

As Bob and I loaded the truck trailer with empty boxes, we listened to his Silvertone white plastic Sears & Roebuck radio. Mr. Gibson was pitching one of his best games. Bob said Mr. Gibson always pitched his best on a blinding hot summer day.

The inside of the metal truck trailer was so hot we couldn't touch its sides without scorching our hands. I could see heat waves in the air as I looked into the dark trailer. Inside, it felt like a blast furnace and sweat was gushing down our faces, arms and chests. To create a cool breeze, Bob opened the narrow side door of the trailer. It created a cross breeze that flowed through the trailer that dried our sweat and cooled us immediately. Even in 100-degree heat, the opened door helped—a lot.

We spent many Sunday afternoons playing in the Kroger trailers filled with Charmin, Kellogg's and Green Giant cardboard boxes, but opening the side door never occurred to us. We didn't want any of our parents to inadvertently see us playing in the trailers.

On that hot, miserable afternoon, just as Bob opened the trailer's side door, Mr. Gibson struck out the last batter for a Cardinal win. As Gibson struck out the last batter, a wild idea snapped into my head—SNAP—like a fastball slapping the leather of my catcher's mitt.

Instantly, I knew exactly how to trap Booger and Butch for some much-deserved payback.

I was extremely excited about the nasty and mean trick I had in mind, but I didn't dare tell Bob. He was just too nice of a guy. He would worry that we would get caught or worse yet, hurt.

My plan was brilliant and I couldn't wait to tell Joey and the guys so I said goodbye to Bob and jumped off of the loading dock. As I ran away, Bob tried to give me a quarter, which would've bought me an ice cream cone and three games of pinball, but I was in too much of a hurry to get to the Clubhouse. I shouted thanks back over my shoulder though. I could see Bob shaking his head slowly from side to side smiling.

The stitch in my side was hurting by the time I got to the Clubhouse, and I was winded from running so fast for so long. Joey, Dave and Rusty were fiddle farting around playing mumblety-peg with their pocketknives. We had a special area to play mumblety-peg next to the Clubhouse where the grass had been worn down to dirt. All we did was lightly wet the dirt down with some water so our knives could easily stick in it. Most of us carried pocketknives that we found lying around our homes or ones we got from our uncles or dads when they replaced their old pocketknives with new ones.

We played lots of versions of pocketknife mumblety-peg. I tried to interrupt Joey and Rusty who had just started playing my favorite mumblety-peg game. It is called 'Indian Stretch.' They told me to hold my idea while they finished their game so they could concentrate.

We play 'Indian Stretch' by facing each other and standing about two feet apart. Our feet are spread about shoulder width apart, but our feet are fixed and flat on the ground. The goal is to stretch the other guy so far that he loses his balance and falls down.

To see who throws first, we flip our knives underhand high into the air, watch it slowly flip and then we see which knife sticks in the ground best.

There are various unwritten rules that govern how good a knife has been stuck into the ground. We measure how deep the blade stabs into the dirt, the size of knife blade, and how many fingers can be placed between the blade and the ground, the more fingers the better. The guy judged to have the best 'stick' gets to go first in the next round.

The guy who throws first has a definite advantage so a lively powwow about whose knife sticks best always follows the "see whom goes first" throws. The powwow is as passionate and fiery as a court of law and carries the same weight.

We use this same powwow process to settle all of our arguments and disagreements. Every important and contentious issue like, "Is the guy safe in baseball, is the guy fouled in basketball, or is the guy out of bounds in football?" are settled with a passionate and fiery powwow. Naturally, everyone watching or participating feels qualified to be the judge and jury, and is therefore intent to sway everyone to his findings and verdict. The discussions are always loud and frenzied.

When enough opinions are heard, a democracy of witnesses proclaims the final decision with the ultimate threat "if you don't like it, go home." At that point, the only option a player has, if he has lost the debate, is to quit in protest. However, a sore loser a.k.a. cry baby, whiner, wienie, momma's boy, or other slanderous insult is always taunted and harassed mercilessly by the entire group the rest of the day. So agreeing with the group is the best resolution—unless you are ready to go home anyway. The only exception to this rule of law is if you own the only baseball, basketball or football that is being used that day. In those cases, unless everyone is ready to quit, the owner is grudgingly given his way. As kids, it doesn't matter; all is forgiven by the next day anyway, when a new game is afoot.

The strategy for Indian Stretch is fairly direct: make a guy stretch until he loses balance and moves his feet, or falls to the ground. A guy throws his knife in the ground so it sticks to the right or left of the other player. The player who didn't throw has to keep one foot in place and flat on the ground, and then stretch his other foot to the knife that was just stuck in the dirt. The goal is to make the other guy do the splits until he falls.

After the player stretches to where the other guy's knife is stuck, it is his turn to stick his knife in such a way as to stretch the other guy's legs apart. The guy has to stick his knife in the dirt to make the other guy stretch. If a guy cannot throw a qualified stick the other guy doesn't move. Where you throw your knife depends on how far you are stretched and in which direction. A guy is always disqualified if he sticks his knife into the other player's foot or leg, whether it is an accident or not even if there isn't much blood.

Rusty threw first and gambled with a long arching underhand pitch that flipped 270-degrees and stuck in the dirt about six feet from Joey's left foot. It was a lucky throw. All of us laughed, Joey winced and the game was instantly over. Joey didn't even try to make the stretch or argue.

Impatient to be heard, I blurted out, "I know how we can trap Butch and Booger for some payback!" "Tell us while we play Mumblety-peg," said Joey as we all sat down in the dirt, knee-to-knee to face each other in a tight circle. Mumblety-peg required more skill and caused more pain than Indian Stretch.

It doesn't matter who goes first in Mumblety-peg. You have to stick your knife in the dirt about fifty different ways and nobody ever completes the cycle without missing. It always takes lots of turns and at least a drop of blood to win the game. The game starts when one guy sticks his knife into the dirt with a simple throw. If it sticks he continues his turn by flipping his pocketknife up in the air with a backward flip that has to stick. If it does, it is still his turn. If his knife doesn't stick; it is the next guy's turn. After the backward flip, you throw salt and pepper throws from your clenched fists. Next come the dreaded flips off of your body parts.

The best pocketknife to throw in Mumblety-peg is balanced with enough weight to stick in the ground and a very sharp point so that it easily sticks in the dirt. The painful challenges are that you have to balance your pocketknife on its point onto your fingertips, elbow and knees and then flip it into the dirt. After the pocketknife is painfully poised on its point onto your body part, you flip your knife using your index finger, which is placed at the other end of the pocketknife. Ideally, the pocketknife flips one-time before it sticks into the dirt. We all dread playing Mumblety-peg but I guess we dread being called "chicken", "yellow" or a "wienie" more. At least that's why I play.

By the end of the game, I was really sorry that all I had was my old Cub Scout knife. It was too heavy with all of its extra blades and gadgets and it poked holes in my skin from its sheer weight, plus the blades were too wide to stick easily.

By the end of the game, which Joey won, I told everybody my plan to trap Booger and Butch like rats. The guys were laughing and rolling all over the ground because they thought it was such a great idea. Immediately, Joey called a war council and we started talking about how we could execute my plan.

The first thing we did was pinky swear ourselves to top secrecy. We considered a blood oath, which was okay with me because I was already bleeding on my knee from mumblety-peg, but the other guys didn't want to cut themselves. So we just promised each other that we wouldn't tell our other friends, brothers, sisters, mothers, or dads anything about our plans.

The second thing we did was give my plan a name. There was a lot of bickering and arguing on this point. I wanted to choose the name since it was my idea, but everybody had a special name that they wanted. Dave wanted "The Hammer" because Thor was his favorite comic book hero. Rusty wanted "The Sweat Box" because of an Army movie he watched with his dad. In the end, everybody agreed that I could choose from everybody's best idea. I chose "Rat Trap," which was Joey's suggestion. It was a cool name because Booger and Butch were first-rate rats. Joey had gotten the idea from the *Mousetrap*, game, which a couple of guys had gotten for Christmas last year.

We decided to execute Rat Trap on Sunday because Kroger's is closed and Booger and Butch usually hang outside at the Rexall Drugstore to smoke cigarettes, pitch coins against the wall, and harass the younger kids by taking their money when they stop to buy candy, soda or ice cream.

Rexall is the most strategic place to start Rat Trap. It is in a strip mall of stores that are connected except for one narrow rainwater drain that is between Rexall and Mr. Kessler's clothing store. The strip of stores has a parking lot in front and an alley behind it. Rexall is in the middle and is a short block from Kroger.

Sunday came quickly, and the weather was perfect. It was blazing hot by the time we got home from St. Kevin's church, and it is supposed to reach over 100 degrees by this afternoon. I was so excited about Rat Trap that I don't even look for my friends after church.

My stomach felt like it had butterflies flying around in it throughout Mass. I couldn't concentrate so I kept looking in my Missal at my favorite picture of Michael the Archangel standing with his foot on the head of Lucifer and his sword held high towards heaven.

The only prayer I remember saying at church was to St. Michael. He is the bravest, strongest, and fastest angel of all so I asked him for help. After all, he had thrown the devil out of heaven and I figured that he was our best bet to throw Booger and Butch out of our lives. I just hoped St. Michael was listening.

I wanted to do something that would be remembered forever. I wanted to do something that I could tell my kids about. I wanted to crush the bullies that chased us and beat us up whenever they saw us. I wanted to smash the two guys who twisted our arms behind our backs and punched us in our stomachs when they caught us. I wanted to hurt them so badly that they would leave us alone. I wanted to bury Butch and Booger in a mound of scorching hot cardboard boxes that was as hot as Hell's fires!

It was nearly one o'clock in the afternoon by the time all of us got home from church, ate lunch, and met at Rexall's drugstore. I was so excited that my stomach felt like it was in my chest.

It was a typical July afternoon in St. Louis; bright sun, no clouds in the bright blue sky, and it was already one hundred degrees. Booger and Butch were standing in their regular spots acting loud and obnoxious. They were dressed in well-worn blue jeans with rolled cuffs, black leather belts, and white t-shirts with their *LSMFT* (Lucky Strike Means Fine Tobacco) cigarettes rolled up into the left sleeves of the t-shirts. Butch kept one unlit cigarette behind his right ear all of the time.

They were greasers. They combed their greasy hair into jellyrolls and cussed at everybody including each other. Today, they were strutting in the shade between Rexall and Kessler's beating the younger kids out of their money, playing Pitch, and cussing a blue streak.

Pitch is a simple game where you challenge any number of people to toss their coins against a wall. The person that tosses their coin closest to the wall collects everyone else's coins. There is no limit to the amount of money you can bet. You can pitch any denomination of coin such as a penny, nickel, dime or a quarter. The older guys even pitched half and silver dollars. It isn't pure luck that usually wins at pitch.

Oh sure, a small piece of gravel, a crack in the concrete, a bad bounce, or something else can affect the outcome of your pitch. Usually though it is skill and 'touch' that wins.

Leaners against the wall always win—almost. You should hear the arguing and screaming if there are two leaners at the same time. It might take a half of an hour to settle that kind of argument with all kinds of huffing and puffing, cussing and screaming and probably some in-your-face pushing and shoving too. Players can give odds by using different coin denominations.

I usually pitched coins to get money for pinball, but Booger and Butch were a lot bigger and older. They would take my coins even if they lost so I didn't play with them.

As I walked up to Rexall's door, which had a cartoon of a penguin advertising ice-cold air conditioning, I chuckled because I was sweating. Then, Butch yelled, "Come over here you little punk. Put your money out here on the sidewalk like a man, you little crybaby!"

Seeing me, two younger guys, Georgie and Gerald, who had already lost most of their money, ran into Rexall to spend what money they had left. I'm not sure why, but I made the sign of the cross and whispered a silent prayer.

I had seen some of the best Cardinals' ball players cross themselves when they stepped up to home plate to bat so I figured it couldn't hurt.

All of my friends imitated big league ball players by doing things like spitting make-believe tobacco juice, and grabbing their crotch. I spit too, especially when I chewed *Black Jack* gum. *Black Jack* tastes like licorice and it makes black juice in your mouth. Mom got mad when I grabbed my crotch at a game once so I stopped doing that. No one gets mad when I make the sign of the cross so it had become part of my regular batting routine along with spitting and tapping the dust out of my Keds with my bat.

When Butch saw me cross myself, he said mockingly, "Are you a-scared? Do you think God is going to save you from me twerp?"

"I'm not a-scared," I stammered.

"OHHH, don't scare the little baby, Butch," goaded Booger. "Where is your punk brother and your punk friends, loser? Don't they want to hang out with a little loser like you anymore?"

"Aww leave the little baby alone," taunted Butch, "He's going to get his mommy and she's going to beat you up."

"Whoa, I'm shaking in my sneakers," sneered Booger. "His mommy's so tough she wears Army boots," and with that he pulled out one of his Lucky Strike/*LSMFT* cigarettes and flipped it into his mouth. With his attention diverted for just a second, I stealthily snatched Booger's pack of cigarettes right out of his hand. My quick hands surprised Booger so much that he fell back a little and screamed, "Hey, what are you doing you little turd?"

I screamed, "I'm taking your stinky cigarettes you big punk. What're you and your girlfriend going to do about it?"

I sprinted towards the center of the parking lot clutching Booger's cigarettes in a death grip high in the air so everyone could see.

Booger and Butch stood whomper-jawed and didn't do or say anything as they looked at each other stupidly. They were in total shock that one of the little kids would challenge them.

Joey objected to me challenging Booger and Butch by myself, but he was my big brother and was always worried about me. True, my plan's details weren't quite worked out, but they weren't as flimsy as wet toilet paper. I always counted on my speed and I was always looking for an opportunity to show off my zip-zap-zoom speed and daring.

Details, schmeee—tails, too much thinking makes my head hurt. All I had to do was get them mad as hornets so they'd chase me and not get caught.

"Give them back before I smash you, punk!" threatened Booger as he slowly scooted toward me, trying to act cool.

"Want these, you little girl? Why don't you beg me," I crowed as I crumpled Booger's Lucky Strikes, and dropped them onto the sizzling hot asphalt and ground them with the right toe of my well-worn, white, high top Ked.

"You're dead meat!" bawled Booger as he sprinted towards me. His face was blister red, his eyes were bulging, and his mouth was wide open as he charged me chugging like a freight train.

That's when I realized I should've thought through the details better. I was terrified of them and I doubted my Rat Trap plan for the first time.

Nervous sweat was spraying out of every pore of my body like our neighbor Frank's lawn sprinkler. My salty sweat was running into my eyes and my sweat burned. Nervously, I took my Cardinals cap off, looked at my Stan Musial flip card in the hatband, folded the cap's bill in half, and stuffed it into my back pocket like I did when I was running the bases. I took a big gulp of air; spit a big gob of cotton spit on the asphalt and stared at Booger and Butch as they circled me. I was determined to not let them catch me.

I was surprised at Booger's speed and quickness. He was five years older than me and he seemed pretty darn fast as he put me in his sights and barreled down.

After a minute of him trying to catch me by himself, Butch started to help corral me. He was just as crazed as Booger and I got twice as nervous and twice as sweaty.

They ran in patterns to trap me between them, but I was always able to dodge them just at the last moment before they grabbed my arms, shirt or neck. Butch caught my hand once, but I was so sweaty I slipped his grip. They were able to block my escape, but they couldn't catch me.

After a few more minutes of running, I was more exhilarated than scared. Truth be told, I was excited at the prospect of getting caught with only my speed and cunning to save me. I got into a rhythm as I ran as fast as I could, dodging and feinting. They were becoming more and more frustrated and angry.

When I got Booger and Butch on either side of me, I ran right between them and escaped towards the alley. They almost ran smack-dab-head-on into each other as they both missed grabbing me at the last second.

I ran around the end store near Ashby Road and reached the alley. I was feeling pretty cocky and yelled over my shoulder, "Come on girls. Can't you catch me?"

My plan was to get them to follow me up the alley to the Rat Trap. I wasn't afraid anymore. Nothing would stop them, they were furious at me.

It would've been wise at that very moment to remember Grandma's saying, "Don't count your chickens before they hatch."

My adrenaline rush was so strong I didn't even look over my shoulder to make sure they were still chasing me. I simply ran around the end store and started running up the alley towards the Kroger loading dock, which was at the other end of the alley. I heard Booger calling me names and yelling stuff, so I knew he was chasing me.

After exploring lots of alleys in St. Ann and south St. Louis, there are certain characteristics I expect to see in an alley. The first is that every alley has at least two ends. The second is that families build high fences with gates that sometimes lock when their yards back up to the alleys. People don't want strangers to easily get into their yards. Lastly, there are lots of nooks and crannies that are great hiding spots in alleys.

I was smiling as I ran up the alley until I turned around and saw Booger kind of chasing me. He had a big Cheshire Cat smile on his face. Confused, I turned back toward Kroger and what I saw stopped me cold. I was trapped.

Butch was standing in the middle of the narrow alley between Kroger's loading dock and me. He was waving to me and said, "Looks like we trapped a rat in the alley, Booger!"

I stood frozen stiff in the July heat. Not thinking through the schmeee-tails, I overlooked the rainwater drain between Rexall and Kessler's. Butch gambled that I would turn into the alley so instead of following me, he took the rainwater drain passage and trapped me.

My mind raced trying to think of some way to escape. Those two smirking creeps closed their trap a little more with each step they took towards me. Winded, I was fresh out of ideas. All of the yards backing up to the alley had big bushes, high fences and locked gates. There wasn't any way that I could jump a fence before they got me. It was Sunday so all of the stores had their alley doors locked. My only hopes were the ends of the alley and Booger and Butch were blocking them. The greatest plan I had ever dreamed up had backfired, and I was trapped like a rat.

Quietly, my brother stood up on the Kroger dock and yelled, "Why don't you big jerks pick on somebody your own size?"

Joey was always around when I needed him; he was after all, my big brother and my best friend. I was relieved when I saw him standing up there on the dock staring at them.

"Look Booger, his big sister's getting mad. Why don't we break this little pip-squeak in half first, then we'll slap his big sister around for opening her big yap," yelled Butch as he waved his fist towards Joey.

"Not hardly," Joey yelled in his best John Wayne imitation as he launched a rock about half the size of a baseball at Butch's head, "Why don't you eat this rock for lunch first Butch!" Then Joey yelled at me, "Get up here quick, Mick!"

Have you ever noticed how big brothers and sisters are always annoying you by telling you what to do? Well today, I didn't care that my All-Star pitcher-brother with an arm like Bob Gibson was being bossy by telling me what to do.

Distracted by the rock launched at his head, Butch looked away from me for a split second to make sure Joey's rock wasn't going to split his skull. When he did, I bolted past him so fast that he didn't see me until I clambered up the loading dock and stood next to Joey. We were both laughing at them as they chased us and scrambled onto the Kroger loading dock.

Joey and I had run into the Kroger truck trailer that Bob and I had carefully loaded with neatly stacked cardboard boxes. As we ran through the trailer, we pulled down all of the neatly stacked cardboard boxes so that Butch and Booger had to climb over the boxes to get to us. Those boxes gave us the few extra seconds that we needed.

The moment Booger and Butch ran into the trailer, Rusty and Dave climbed onto the loading dock from underneath the trailer where they had been hiding. Once there, they slammed and latched the two big doors at the backend of the trailer where everyone had entered. This trapped the four of us inside and made the trailer as dark as the sewers, but it sure wasn't cool.

The trailer had sat in the sun all day long. It was as hot as an oven—everything felt hot, the sides of the trailer, the boxes, and the ceiling. Even the floor was hot. We were as soaked as if we had been playing in a hose. Sweat was pouring out of every pore of our bodies. Our noses, chins, arms, necks, backs and even our legs were sweaty. It was boiling hot.

The moment Rusty and Dave slammed the doors shut, Butch and Booger frantically screamed, "Open the doors you little turds or we're going to kill your girl friends in here!"

You could feel their fear as Joey and I escaped through the narrow side door of the trailer. The sunlight from the open door must have been blinding as it gave false hope to Booger and Butch for just a split second that they could escape. We had wedged the door closed with a piece of cardboard to hide our escape. Once outside, we latched the side door as fast as we could. It was almost too late. One of the guys slammed his body heavily against the door. I couldn't tell if he groaned because he was hurt or because he realized he was trapped.

Exhilarated and scared at the same time, I couldn't believe we had actually trapped the meanest neighborhood bullies in the Kroger trailer—just like I planned.

The moment they realized they were trapped, they started viciously snarling and growling like rabid dogs. For a brief moment, I actually felt sorry for them, as they threatened cussed, kicked, and pounded the walls and doors of the trailer as loud as they could. After 10 minutes or so of steaming heat, their voices grew hoarse and weak. They pleaded with us to be set free through a small hole we had opened for fresh air by chaining the doors shut on the end. Although the trailer and the cardboard muffled their screams, they were crazed and I was feeling more afraid of them now than before we had trapped them.

Torture was our first impulse for revenge, but we couldn't do much more than we already had. We pounded on the walls of the trailer and yelled jeers and taunts back at them, which released our anxiety and energy.

I yelled, "Who's got who, now—you big punks? You're not so tough now are you? I better be careful, cause big bad Booger and Butch are going to kill me," and then we laughed and I pounded the trailer loudly.

Rusty and Dave had made a 'special present' that they hid in the trailer for Butch and Booger. It was a wooden crate full of rotted fruits and vegetables that stunk to high heaven.

The guys had dug some rotted food out of the trash bin that was sitting next to the trailer. The fruits and vegetables had been lying out in the sun for the past couple of days. Kroger employees threw all of the old food in the trash bin. You could usually find a couple of rats there too so you had to be careful, when you grabbed something.

After an hour or so of yelling and throwing rocks and green apples at the trailer, we started getting bored by torturing our captives. We had done a great job capturing them, but we hadn't planned what to do with them once they were our prisoners.

Joey silently called a meeting by motioning with his hands to us. Then he loudly said, "Hey Butch and Booger, it's too hot out here, we have to go home and eat, so we'll see you guys later."

"You better not leave us in here, you better let us out or we are really going to kill you when we get out," one of them threatened.

"Yeah, right," said Joey "You're so tough, four punks just trapped you and now we're going to leave you here until you're so hungry you eat that rotted food."

"It stinks really bad in here. You better let us out— right now," one of them moaned. None of us even bothered to answer him. We were bored.

To answer the silence, they bawled even louder while we met in the shade under the loading dock to discuss our options. Under the loading dock wasn't a very nice place to be either. It was cooler, but it smelled just like the rotted food in the trailer so we didn't want to stay any longer than we had to stay.

We whispered so they couldn't hear us.

"Let's kill them, Joey," said Rusty half seriously; "They almost broke my arm once twisting it behind my back."

"We're not going to kill them Rusty. We just want to scare them so they leave us alone," said Joey.

"Boy, they're really mad. Any of you guys got any ideas what we should do now that we have them trapped?"

"Let's keep them in there. They're always taking my money and punching me every time they see me. Let's roast them like a turkey!" I said.

"How hot do you think it is in there?' asked Dave, "Maybe we should let them out. Do you think they might die?"

"I hope they do," said Rusty.

"Aww, they're not going to die," said Joey "We play in those trailers all of the time. Do we die? We have them right where we want them. Let's not get scared."

"Let's leave them in the trailer and let them get hauled away tomorrow," I said. "If we let them out, they'll pick on us because they think we're scared of them."

"Maybe we should bring them some food, so they don't die," said Dave.

"Would you stop with the dying, Dave? They're not going to die. Stay cool," laughed Joey. "Speaking of cool, it's too hot out here. Let's go buy an ice cream cone at Rexall and sit in the air-conditioning." So, we strolled down to Rexall proud as peacocks.

I was becoming philosophical over what to do with Butch and Booger. They reminded me of bugs.

We captured bees and lightning bugs all summer. It was more exciting capturing them than it was fun torturing them. I would shake the jars until the bees got so dizzy and looked dead. Then I would open the jars and they would fly away when they got undizzy.

It was the same with lightning bugs. At the beginning of the summer, when I first saw them at night, I would put them in jars with a few blades of grass or rip their lights off and wear them as rings, but the novelty wore off pretty quickly. After a night or two, I wouldn't even trap them. But, they weren't bugs, and I didn't trust Booger and Butch to leave us alone. They were more dangerous now than before.

After we licked and slurped our fifteen-cent ice cream cones, I got butterscotch fudge; we decided to go into the bowling alley to play some pinball where it was also air-conditioned.

Ray was the owner of the bowling alley. He'd let us hangout as long as we spent money on soda, food, or pinball. Oddly, we never bowled because it cost fifteen-cents a game and shoes were another dime. It was too expensive.

In the alley, we ran into Billy and Johnny and we told them how we had captured Butch and Booger. They thought we were lying so we bet them twenty-five-cents and swore them to secrecy.

We crept up to the trailer as quiet as spiders, and then all at once, we all pounded on the side of the trailer as loud as we could to stir up Butch and Booger, just like I shook the jars with bees.

We didn't hear a sound. At first we thought they were dead or they had escaped. Then we heard a few groans and moans. We were shocked to hear the difference in their voices. They were a whole lot tamer after being trapped a couple of hours in a dark, hot trailer full of smelly boxes, thinking they wouldn't ever get out.

Butch pleaded, "Come on guys, please let us out, it's hotter than Hell in here. We have to get out. We're going to die in here."

"Yeah," Booger said, "I'm hungry. You caught us. We've learned our lesson—now let us out—please! We won't bother you guys anymore. We promise."

"Sure Booger, like we believe *YOU*," I yelled sarcastically.

Well nobody believed Butch or Booger for a second and everybody was silently shaking his head 'No,' to each other.

Billy was shaking his head 'No' and saying, "No way, man, don't let those guys out. You can't trust them now, no way. Those punks will beat us up the first chance they get."

"They'll kill us. Don't trust them," Rusty said.

"They might die," said Dave.

"So what!" said Rusty.

Then Joey said, "We'll let you guys know what we're going to do after dinner," and then he waved us away from the trailer and we walked home for supper. As we walked away, they were whimpering for mercy. Deep down, I think we were all scared of them, I know I was.

We met at the Clubhouse after dinner to discuss our options. As usual, Joey had already made up our minds, he just hadn't told us yet. He decided that we, meaning he, needed to negotiate an uneasy peace with Butch and Booger. The rest of us wanted some of the cash they had taken from us over the years, but we all agreed Joey should negotiate for us once we got to the Kroger trailer.

We weren't ready for what we found at the loading dock when we got there. Billy was getting kids from the neighborhood to pay him money to see Butch and Booger trapped in the trailer like animals in the zoo. I admired Billy and was mad at myself for not thinking of it first.

"What're you doing, Billy, you didn't help catch them?" I grumbled.

"Yeah, I know. I'm just making some money that's all. I'll pay you guys the quarter from our bet," he laughed.

"You better give me some money," groused Rusty, "I put my life on the line catching those guys."

Georgie, Gerald, and everybody else that had been bullied by Butch and Booger were hanging around throwing rocks at the trailer and yelling at them. Joey just laughed and climbed up onto the loading dock.

It was getting a little cooler, but it was still in the high 90s and several hours before sunset. Even the concrete loading dock was still hot to touch. There wasn't any breeze out at all and we were all as sticky as sweet cinnamon rolls from sweating all day.

Joey told us to keep everybody away from the dock as he laid down on it in the little bit of shade that was there. He spoke quietly into the gapped space between the chained trailer doors that we had left for air. There was a little space that allowed us to see one mouth and a set of ears.

Nobody but Joey and them could hear what was actually being said. Butch and Booger were eager to negotiate, but none of us trusted them to keep their promises. After a few minutes of talking, we heard Joey say toughly, "That's not good enough. You ain't getting out," and then he jumped off the dock and came over to us.

We were anxious to hear what was being said. Joey told us that he wanted a secret from Butch and Booger to bind their promise, but they wouldn't tell him anything really good. He wanted to know something they had done that was illegal, but they didn't trust him not to tell the police.

"Man, that trailer really stinks. You guys did a great job with the stink bomb," chuckled Joey. We all laughed, but we stopped cold when Joey told us what he had promised them. He told them that he wouldn't tell any of us their secret. He told them that he'd be the only guy who would know it unless they bullied us again, and then he'd tell the police.

This made us feel a little distrustful of Joey. We wanted to know the secret too. Joey explained that Butch and Booger said that Billy bringing all of the kids proved that we couldn't keep a secret. Joey agreed that Billy had messed up and promised that he would only tell the police their secret if they touched any of us ever again.

"What about some money?" Rusty asked.

"I'll see," said Joey and with that he climbed back on to the dock to continue our negotiations. Twenty minutes later, we saw one of the bullies' hands pass something under the trailer's doors to Joey.

We heard Joey say, "It's a deal. I'll be back in a few minutes." He jumped down and walked over to us with a wad of dollar bills and some change in his hands with a smile as wide as his face. Joey had struck a deal and we were smiling too as soon as we saw the money.

Joey divided the money evenly among us, but he gave me the extra half dollar and told everybody to go back to the Clubhouse so that he could release our prisoners.

I acted like I left with Billy, Rusty and Dave, but I hid in some bushes so that I could make sure they didn't jump Joey. Butch and Booger shuffled out of the trailer. Their clothes were soaked from sweating, and their greasy and sweaty heads were hung in shame as they nodded towards Joey and trudged away from Kroger's parking lot.

After they left, I ran over to Joey and asked him their deep, dark secret. He told me that they admitted that they had started the fire behind the furniture store last month.

"We know that Joey, we saw them running away," I said disgustedly.

"Yeah, that's why I know they're telling the truth, but you ought to hear the rest of the stuff," said Joey with a laugh and a big grin.

"Well tell me, Joey," I said, "Tell me."

"I will later Mickey, let's go find the guys and play some hide and seek, " he said as we trotted off towards the Clubhouse.

I never told Bob what we did to Booger and Butch in the trailer, but I don't think he would've been surprised. He always said, "You sure are a good worker Mr. Mickey."

Chapter 12

Sultry Days of Summer

During a sultry summer day, getting to someplace cool is our first thought and our number one priority. We don't have air conditioning in our home and neither do most of my friends. When St. Louis thermometers hit one hundred degrees, it feels like we are condemned to Hell. We go limp, and feel overpowered, exhausted, and ready for a nap. After just 10 minutes in the wilting heat, we are barely able to move. During the nighttime, as I lay there sweating in my bed in just my pajama bottoms without any sheets or blankets, I dream about having an air conditioner in our home. I'm sure heaven is air-conditioned.

Home air conditioners in St. Ann are as rare as cool days in July. Only the King family has a window air conditioner on our street, and Mrs. King doesn't feel very generous when it comes to sharing her air-conditioned living room with a bunch of sweaty boys. So, when the heat is more than we can bear, we pray for relief and then seek it somewhere else, someplace cool.

Our creativity thrives during a St. Louis heat wave. We spend the entire day trying to get out of the heat. We use a variety of techniques to escape the sweat-drenching, sun-scorched days that turns us into roasted Boris Karloff mummies.

On those red-hot summer days, our mouths get so dry we can't spit anything but cotton. So, we grab mouthfuls of water anywhere we can find them—neighbors' garden hoses, stores' water fountains, or we knock on people's doors and beg for ice water. One day I was so thirsty, I licked the salty sweat off my dirty arm, but it tasted so awful I never tried it again.

We usually start a scorching day by hanging out in each other's basements reading comics or trading and flipping baseball cards until we get bored or our mothers' get tired of us and kick us out.

Then we wander around until we are able to sneak into an air-conditioned store like Kroger's or W.T. Grants to read newly released comic books without spending any money. We read Superman, Spiderman, Thor, Fantastic Four, and Batman comics until some meddling clerk finds us lying under a clothes rack or behind some shelves and kicks us out of the store. After we get kicked out, we move to our next location. We are a band of traveling gypsies looking for relief from the heat.

Another popular spot is Kroger's loading dock next to the butchers. We stand on the concrete dock watching the butchers cut up meat and let the cool air from the bloody ice packed around the dead chickens and the bloody sides of beef and pork drift over our sweaty bodies. The butchers don't bother us, but there isn't any place to sit or lay down, so we wander to someplace new after we cool off.

When we are lucky enough to find some abandoned soda bottles, we take them to the stores and cash them in for their two-cent deposits. Then we hangout in the smoky air-conditioned St. Ann bowling alley to play pinball or go to Rexall Drug and buy ice cream cones or fountain sodas until we are out of money. We will do anything—just to get cool.

If it isn't too, too hot and it is in the morning, we chase the Pevely Dairy milk truck throughout our neighborhood. After stalling us a while, the driver bribes us to leave him alone with a few handfuls of chopped up ice that is packed around the bottles of milk. The chunks of ice are always a little dirty and taste like metal, but most importantly, they are wet and ice cold.

If the heat hasn't zapped all of our energy, we wander down to the shady banks of Cold Water Creek and grab tadpoles or fish for crawdads with bacon on a string.

We rarely tell our parents where we are going, but if we say we were going to the library—there are never any questions. It doesn't matter if it's cold, hot, raining or if there is a tornado coming, the answer is always "Okay. Be good."

All of us, except Joey, don't particularly like going to the library because it's a long walk, and it doesn't have any comic books to read. On Saturday mornings, the library shows a good free movie. The library isn't an awful place. It's just that it reminds me of school, and I'm always expected to learn something whenever I go to the library—just like school.

The library is as quiet as a classroom, and the librarians hover over us like the nuns the whole time we are there. The librarians put their long, pointy index fingers up to their lips so often that it looks like they are constantly picking their noses.

Librarians make more noise "Shush-shing" us than we make whispering and giggling when we show each other stuff in books that we find.

The thing that I enjoy most about visiting the library on a searing summer day is taking a nap on its frigid tile floor. It is heaven to feel the cold tile floor on my sweaty bare legs and arms, but I have to be careful not to get caught by the meddlesome librarians or I will get kicked out.

My favorite spot to lie down and nap is under the staircase by the newspaper rack. The hanging newspapers do a great job of screening me as I lay between them and the wall. Almost numb from the cold floor, I usually fall asleep reading the colored comic pages of the *St. Louis Post-Dispatch*.

Today, it is very, very, very hot and I am very, very, very tired; so I plan to take a nap as soon as I get to the library, while Joey looks for some big book about Napoleon or somebody else to check out.

Whenever we go to the library, it's our ritual to first rummage through the trash dumpster behind the library. We always look through trash dumpsters, when we see one. I don't know why we always scour the dumpsters for treasure, but we do. It's like blinking or breathing, we just do it.

When we see a big metal trash dumpster, one of us will immediately crawl in to see if there is something neat-o and cool that we can keep or trade.

The stuff that we find is free so it doesn't have to be valuable; it just has to be interesting. We can always find some use for it or make stories up about it. Some of the trashier treasures we have found are the used fireworks from the Optimists' Fourth of July display, rotted vegetables and fruit for food fights, empty cardboard boxes, old books and clothes, and broken stuff like toys and furniture.

The most valuable treasure I ever found was in Carafoil's furniture store dumpster. It was a scratched up chair that didn't have a seat. Dad and Mom turned it into a family heirloom. Dad painted it white and then painted blue antiquing and gold pin stripes. Mom replaced its seat with a needlepoint cushion. It was an instant antique, as it looked French and quite exotic.

Today, Charlie was the first one of us to dive into the dumpster, and almost immediately, we heard him scream at the top of his lungs "Holy cow, here's a picture of a naked lady!"

"What?" We all sang out like a church choir. "Let me see!"

"Holy mackerel," Charlie squealed, "There's a bunch of naked ladies' pictures in here." Well none of us needed any more coaxing than that as the four us dove headfirst into the dumpster like a pod of dolphins.

We moved so fast, you would have thought that stinky old dirty dumpster was a pool of ice-cold water. If there were pictures of naked women, no one wanted to be left out.

"I've never seen anything like this," said Joey dreamily lying on his back at the bottom of the trash bin, gaping at a doozy of a photo of a glitzy young woman draped over a sofa, naked as a jaybird.

"Me neither," agreed Billy, "I'm taking them home."

"No you're not Billy, they're mine," declared Charlie.

"Bbbuuuttt," Billy stammered, "You ain't old enough to look at these Charlie."

Well with that comment, we all doubled up and roared with laughter. Billy was the same age as Charlie. I was laughing so hard that my sides actually ached, and I had to cross my legs so I wouldn't pee in my pants. Even Billy burst out laughing when he realized how goofy it sounded. Heck, Billy was turning the magazine pages so fast that Joey threatened to call the fire department if he didn't slow down. Although it was the scorching sun than burned our skin, it was the magazines that made our blood sizzle.

Charlie was right. No one could argue that fine point of kid-law which clearly asserts, 'Finders keepers.'

Charlie was the rightful owner of the girlie magazines and all of the guys in the dumpster envied him and his newfound status and treasure. Everybody wanted to be Charlie's best friend today.

Thinking it through, Billy backed off his claim and gently suggested, "Well you better find someplace better than this dumpster to look at your magazines or you're going to get caught Charlie."

Everyone nodded agreement. Billy was right. It was time to vamoose with Charlie's newfound treasures. Everyone naturally turned to Joey for an idea and got real quiet so they could hear as Joey hatched our plan.

"We need to find a bag for these magazines. Anybody see a bag in here?" In an instant, we were a mob of mad rats scrambling through the dumpster searching for a bag to carry Charlie's loot.

"Here's a bag but it's got ketchup all over and some lunch in it. Anybody see one cleaner?" asked Billy.

Nobody seemed to think we were doing anything wrong. So I felt compelled to ask the questions that everybody should've been thinking, "Is it a sin to look at pictures of naked girls?"

"What're you, a priest? We're not kidnapping the girls. We're in a dumpster, Mickey. These are just magazines that's all, Mickey," growled Billy,

"Yeah, it ain't a sin. Dad's got girlie magazines, it's okay to look," agreed Charlie, "As long as we don't show them to little kids."

Looking for reassurance, I looked to my big brother, "What do you think Joey?"

"It's okay, Mickey. Here's a clean bag, put them in here guys," said Joey.

"Make sure you get them all," commanded Billy as he wildly dug through more trash nervously looking for more magazines. He became ecstatic when he found another. "This one is mine!"

"Where are we going Joey?"

"Down to the creek under the Red Bridge. It's a lot cooler there," said Joey.

Joey could hatch a plan quicker than a hen could lay an egg. His mind was always working, and his plan was hatched while the rest of us dreamed about the pinup girls. When Joey had good ideas, everybody generally accepted them as their own. It isn't that Joey was tough or bossy, but he just always seemed to get his own way. I don't ever remember seeing Joey in a fistfight.

He had a different style than the other guys. He was nice to everybody. He always listened to the other guys brag without bragging and he always had a quiet, confident smile. His confidence made everybody else confident, and when it came to deciding what to do, Joey quietly did exactly what he wanted, and we usually followed. Today, we had to be especially careful. If our moms found out or saw us with these magazines, we would be grounded for the rest of the summer.

It was about 20 degrees cooler in the shade under the Red Bridge, but it got about a hundred degrees hotter once we opened that bag of girlie magazines. We hooted and howled like a pack of wild wolves every time one of the guys would hold up a magazine to show us a new girl. "Wow, look at her, she's unbelievable, she's beautiful!" we'd sing in unison.

There weren't any grown-ups under the Red Bridge. It was our private world. When we hung out under the bridge, some of the guys would cuss and a few even smoked cigarettes that they snitched from their parents. We would throw big rocks from the bank into the deep part of the creek, and try to catch another guy unawares with a big splash. It was my favorite place to hangout. You could say anything and nobody could hear you but the other guys.

I was suddenly shocked when I saw a picture of a girl that looked exactly like Streak's blonde girlfriend that I saw on his motorcycle. In the magazine, she was straddling a chrome-plated, chopped motorcycle, painted cherry red. The color of the motorcycle matched the color of her bikini bottom. I felt myself blush as I ogled her.

Truth be told, I felt pretty sinful at that particular moment, even if it wasn't a sin to be looking at pictures of naked girls. And for the first time since Charlie found the magazines, I read the words under her photograph hoping to find the name of the girl on the motorcycle. There it was, right under her photograph, 'Lola Lipps takes this cherry, chopped Harley for a spin around the block.'

This revelation took my breath away. The fact that I knew a celebrity was like a dream. Just as I was about to rip Lola's picture out of the magazine so the other guys wouldn't see her, Billy ripped the magazine from my hands, "What are you looking at Suzie?"

It only took only a moment for Billy to recognize Streak's girlfriend. Then he yelled out to all of the other guys and they rushed over to see her photograph. Ever since I had seen her that day, I had a secret crush on her, but I didn't tell anybody else because I knew they would just laugh at me. Hearing what all the guys were saying about her smashed me as flat as a pancake. It was a nightmare. The girl of my dreams was everybody's dream girl.

Deflated, I just wanted to go home. I wasn't having fun anymore. I didn't care that the rest of the guys wanted to hang out looking at Lola and the rest of the girls. Dejected, I went home to my basement to stay cool, and reread some of my favorite Spiderman comics. Later, I fell asleep on the cold concrete basement floor.

I don't know what ever happened to Lola's pictures. Joey said they hid the magazines under the bridge, but when they went back later the magazines were gone. The guys thought Billy secretly took them and sold them. I didn't know and I didn't care.

Chapter 13

Thinking Inside the Box

We love to escape our modern, suburban lives to travel to our distant worlds of 'make believe' and we have lots of help. Our black and white televisions and Technicolor movies spark our imaginations. We read books and comics too but it is a lot more fun to watch Fess Parker play Davy Crockett on a television screen than it is to read a book about Davy Crockett even if it has color pictures.

When our moms tell us to "turn off the idiot box," and they kick us outside; we like to buckle up our Fanner-Fifty holsters to play. I prefer cross-draw action. Then, we mount our "play" horses and ride around the neighborhood playing make-believe cowboys. Although the guys on my street like to play cowboys best, other guys on other streets, like Jimmie, who live a street over on St. Philip, love to play make-believe Army or war.

On St. Stephen, we imagine that we are different cowboys like the Lone Ranger, Cisco Kid, Wyatt Earp, Roy Rogers, Rowdy Yates or any John Wayne movie character. Then we create our own adventure plot, which ultimately necessitates the timely demise of some really bad guys. Jimmie and I agree about John Wayne. He is the best. John Wayne plays cowboys and modern Army soldiers in the movies we watch. I think I've seen all of his movies. God bless John Wayne.

Like most of the other guys, I have a whole arsenal of different play guns. I have cowboy pistols and a rifle, army guns, and even an Elliott Ness snub-nose .38 Special with a rubber Untouchable shoulder holster. When I want to play 'Army,' I go play with Jimmie at his house.

Jimmie likes to play make-believe Army games inspired by John Wayne movies, and he has a PT boatload full of real army equipment from his dad. He has belts, and helmets, along with an authentic wooden shell box full of toy rifles, machine guns and pistols. Jimmie is ready for a make believe war.

Jimmie's dad must've been a hero in World War II, because he brought a lot of military hardware back from the Pacific that filled his basement. Almost everyone in St. Ann had a concrete basement to store stuff, but most people didn't have finished rooms in their basements.

Jimmie's parents finished and furnished their basement to look just like the upstairs, and they call it a 'rathskeller' not a basement, which gives it an air of distinction. Some families finish their basements to make their small homes larger, but Jimmie's rathskeller is the coolest, and it has special touches that others didn't have. Most important, his rathskeller has a color TV, which is very rare as is his dad's Tiki bar.

When Jimmie's parents have parties, they serve beer, wine or other mysterious concoctions in plastic coconuts. Their rathskeller has the only bumper pool table any of us have ever seen. And if that isn't cool enough, their rathskeller has lots of military medals, patches, and equipment on display. There are American and Japanese flags, maps, swords, helmets, and a locked wooden display case that his dad made. The case holds real pistols, and rifles and a Japanese sword along with some machine gun and artillery shells. The coolest thing by far is an ornately framed painting of a gorgeous blonde woman kneeling on a floor with her hair flowing in the wind. She is wearing a tight one-piece red swimsuit and a big bright smile. Her name, painted across the bottom, is Zsa Zsa. The painting hangs on the rathskeller wall behind the bar along with a bamboo 'Hooch Hut' sign. A soldier that was in the war with Jimmie's dad had painted them, but he had been killed during the war. Zsa Zsa was beautiful and all of us guys imagined she was our girlfriend as we drank our sodas and shot bumper pool in Jimmie's basement.

It was just such an afternoon, when Jimmie came up with a heck of a good idea for a new clubhouse and another club called the 'Aces.' The Aces was the name of Jimmie's dad's Army patrol.

After some prodding and bribing, Jimmie coaxed us outside into the heat to inspect the premises of his proposed clubhouse for the Aces. Jimmie's dad had built a large family room onto the back of their house to make yet more space for his family. Under this family room was a dirt crawl space that was about two and a half feet high. We could crawl into the space through a small, white wooden door that was hidden from the view of people standing in Jimmie's back yard and his neighbors. Jimmie said nobody ever used the door or went into the crawl space.

As we crept up to the door, which was hidden behind a small bush, Jimmie whispered, "Follow me guys, but be quiet or Mom will hear us," and with that he unlatched the door and crawled into the darkness.

I wasn't sure I wanted to crawl into a dark cave again, when a light mysteriously came on inside the crawl space. Next, Jimmie's head popped out of the door like a turtle's with one of his fingers pressed to his lips to keep us quiet. His other hand waved us inside.

Curious, we slithered across the dirt floor after Jimmie while he pulled the strings on two more light bulbs. What had been a dark and foreboding area turned into a well lit, if cramped area. We were as quiet as snakes as we carefully eyeballed the area for varmints. I didn't spot anything but some spiders and roly-polies. The crawl space was surprisingly cool even though there wasn't any breeze. Not surprisingly, it was dusty and we couldn't stand or even really sit up straight. We had to lay all of the time.

After lurking around a while, we heard footsteps as someone walked across the family room floor directly overhead. It was Jimmie's mom or sister. Then she must have sat down in the corner of the room because we heard a little squeak and her footsteps stopped. After a few more moments of silence, we heard Jimmie's sister's happy voice say," Hi Marianne, it's Celeste." Jimmie's sister was in high school and she was *HOT!*

"What're you doing? I'm so bored."

[A few moments of silence]

Sounding exasperated, "I can't. I have to watch my little brat brother this afternoon while Mom goes to Kroger. "

[A long pause of silence then Celeste started her high pitch giggle, which clearly demonstrated she was crazy or in love.]

"Oh yeah, I saw him at the American Legion pool too [giggle], he's dreamy! Did you see all of those muscles and his cute friends? [Giggle] Sheez, I thought I'd die, when those boys came over," [giggle, as she gave this groaning sound.] We could hear Celeste's voice perfectly.

[A few moments of silence]

As Celeste talked to her friend, we looked into each other's extra-large and wide-open eyes. We realized we had hit pay dirt. We could hang in the crawl space and listen to all of Celeste's telephone calls and everything else that happened in the family room without anybody knowing we were there spying on them. It was ingenious. Joey motioned for all of us to crawl to the door quietly. Jimmie turned out the lights on our way out.

After we crawled out of the Aces' Clubhouse, Jimmie motioned for us to follow him. He led us past some large cardboard boxes in the driveway to a patch of taller grass behind his garage that had a few piles of big rocks and bricks. He pulled a metal box out from under one of the piles. Joey and I looked at each other quizzically as Jimmie pulled a corncob pipe and a pouch of tobacco from the box.

"You guys got a whatchamacallit?" Jimmie asked.

"A match?" asked Joey.

"Yeah, a match. You got one? If you do we can smoke my pipe together."

"We don't smoke tobacco, Jimmie. We tried Dad's cigarettes once and we got real sick. Do you smoke?"

"No, I just keep this stuff here in case I want to try it sometime. Dad threw this pipe away because the stem broke and I snitched some of his tobacco."

"It's a cool pipe," I said, as I noted that it looked like a whole corncob stuck in the middle with a stick.

"Thanks, yeah, Dad smokes a corncob pipe just like General MacArthur."

"Hey guys, let's build our own rathskeller under the room," suggested Jimmie, "It'd be cool!"

"Hmm, I have an idea Aces," said Joey as he slapped his hands on his thighs with delight, "Let's take those boxes in Jimmie's driveway and cut them up so we can spread them out on the dirt floor of the clubhouse. It'd be a lot better than crawling in the dirt."

"That's a great idea," I said as I took out my Cub Scout pocketknife and volunteered to do the cutting.

"Roger," saluted Jimmie. All of the guys were experts on the subject of cardboard boxes. We used them for everything and collected them from everywhere. Each cardboard box had its own unique characteristics of size, texture, and strength. Jimmie's boxes were highly prized because they were extra-large and heavy duty. They had been used to hold a new electric washing machine and a new electric dryer that his parents had just bought.

Big appliance boxes are more rare than smaller ones and they are perfect for building tanks to roll down hills, dark mazes and clubhouses. Appliance boxes are also perfect for building slides down steep yards or hills. As we stood in the driveway admiring his boxes, we were tempted to just forget the plan and start playing, but Joey kept us on task. He decided that we needed more boxes for our new clubhouse's floor. So we took a hike to Carafoil's furniture store.

Carafoil's store has a fenced area in the alley to store empty cardboard boxes until the trash truck picks them up. Sometimes it's empty and sometimes, like today, it's full of boxes from sofas, mattresses, chairs and all kinds of appliances. The fenced storage area is about eight feet wide; twenty feet long, and twenty feet high. It holds lots of boxes and none of them are too smashed or broken down yet. They are just thrown in any which way, which makes a tempting maze of paths and hideouts in a cardboard tree house. It's perfect for playing a game that is a combination of tag and hide-n-seek. Seeing them we started scrambling in and around the boxes as fast as we could and like a bunch of squirrels.

Fortunately, we had lots of fun and got real hot and sweaty before some red-faced, angry employee saw us and yelled, "Hey, you kids, what're doing? Get out of there before you get hurt! I'm calling the cops!"

"Yes sir, we are sorry sir," said Joey mockingly, "We just got carried away. We need some boxes for our Clubhouse. May we have some, please?"

"Yeah, okay, get them and get out of there!"

"Yes sir, thank you sir," mocked Joey as we slid out from under the boxes. I climbed down from the top rail, where I was hiding in a chair box to escape being tagged by Jimmie. After we carefully selected our boxes, we took them back to Jimmie's house. Hauling them was no easy task. We had stacked the smaller ones inside of the bigger ones and balanced the biggest one on top of Jimmie's red wagon. Joey pulled, Jimmie pushed and I kept them from sliding off the side.

We got the boxes to Jimmie's house just as his mom drove up. "What are you boys doing? We don't have any room for that big box. We already have two that Dad has to cut up tonight."

Jimmie's mom didn't see the six smaller boxes that we had carefully fit inside the biggest box. "Aww Mom, we just want to play with them for a while, that's all," pleaded Jimmie.

"Well okay, but don't make a big mess."

"We won't Missus Godfrey. We'll clean up the other boxes too so Mister Godfrey doesn't have to do it tonight," promised Joey as he winked to us.

"Well that'd be very nice, thanks Joey," she said with shining admiration.

The second she was inside the house, we went to work cutting the boxes apart and fitting the pieces through the door of the Clubhouse. After another trip to Carafoil's Furniture, we had installed wall-to-wall cardboard floors and built a few walls too, but we were dog-tired, and it was time for dinner so Joey and I left.

Jimmie was really excited about the Aces' new rathskeller, and Missus Godfrey was happy that we had gotten rid of her boxes.

Just as we finished dinner, Jimmie knocked at our front screen door, "Can Joey and Mickey play?" We looked for permission from Dad to leave the table and he nodded. We were excused.

We were hardly out of the door when Jimmie started whispering, "Right after you left, I went in the Aces' rathskeller and heard Celeste on the phone again."

"What was she saying?"

"She's was talking to her boyfriend. She's sneaking out to meet him at the Airway Drive-In Saturday night. She's telling Mom and Dad she's going with Marianne, but Marianne's meeting her boyfriend too!"

"Oh man, that's so cool. You heard the whole thing?"

"Yeah!" crowed Jimmie proudly, "Then, I blackmailed my sister. She said the Aces can go to the

Airway with her and Marianne, Saturday night, if we don't tell anybody about their boyfriends."

"Are you' kidding me?"

"You blackmailed your own sister?"

"Yeah, it was so cool. She wanted to know how I knew, but I didn't squeal."

"Man, this is great. All we have to do is talk our parents into letting us go."

"I don't think Dad will care as long as we pay with our own money," said Joey wryly.

On Saturday nights in the summer, no matter how hot it is, all four-lanes of the St. Charles Rock Road are a bumper-to-bumper parade of honking cars filled with loud, rowdy, and rambunctious kids and families heading to the drive-in theatres.

The Airway Drive-In's three-story tall, smiling, baton twirling, red-haired marching band majorette in white boots leads the parade of cars. She stands at the entrance of the Airway Drive-In and she is lit by colorful spinning bright neon lights.

We actually have two drive-in movie theatres within a half-mile of each other that are packed with people all summer especially on the weekends.

There is the Airway Drive-In and the St. Ann Four Screen Drive-In. The Airway has one super large screen, a roller coaster and a large section of outside stadium seats up front where kids can hang out with their friends and watch the movies—away from their parents. The Four Screen Drive-In has four full-sized movie screens playing two sets of different movies, and a playground with a train for little kids.

Drive-in movies are an important part of our families' lives because they give the whole family an affordable place to escape with their favorite movie stars. Where else can you pay two bucks per car and take your large Catholic family out for a night's entertainment? Nothing is cheaper or cooler on a summer evening.

The Airway is so close to my house. I can climb a couple of the neighborhood's bigger trees or sneak into an open field on the other side of the alley to see the screen. I can watch about a half hour of the Airway's movies without sound, before I have to be in my house to get ready for bed.

Tonight, Celeste is driving the Godfrey's brand-new convertible Rambler. It is a bright gold and the white convertible top is down. The evening is beautifully clear with a cool breeze. The three Aces are sitting in the back seat and the Airway's bright neon lights are reflecting off our scheming, mischievous smiles. It is going to be a night to remember.

As we wait our turn to enter the Airway's large entrance, which is six car lanes wide, I recognize Sergeant Rogers, the policeman directing traffic. His son, Robby, is in my class. He gives me a wave, but he is really busy directing all of the cars. He is holding these large red lights that looked like huge cherry popsicles to direct the cars.

Spending a summer evening at the drive-in movies is always special, but tonight is especially neat-o because we aren't with our parents—for the first time. To save some of our hard-earned money, Mom has popped a whole brown paper grocery sack full of salted popcorn and made a large aluminum Coleman thermos of ice-cold lemonade.

We also brought some old quilted blankets so we can sit on the ground in front of the Rambler. It's more comfortable to sit outside of the car and besides the girls won't hear us scheme. Of course, we can't hear them either.

On the weekends, the Airway shows three movies, but our parents will only let us stay for the first two tonight, which are both comedies. The first movie being shown is *Wheeler Dealers*, starring James Garner, which is okay, but the main feature is *It's A Mad, Mad, Mad, Mad World*, starring every comedian whoever made me laugh, except Red Skelton. My favorite comedian, Jonathan Winters, is in the movie. His crazy characters crack me up.

Once in the drive-in, everyone has different places they want to park their car. Families with kids prefer to be near the concession stand. That way, they can more easily get in and out of their boat-sized cars to take their kids to the bathrooms and buy snacks.

There is always an endless parade of little kids dressed in their pajamas carrying stuffed teddy bears and dolls trudging behind their parents or standing in line as they wait for their turn. Little boys usually go into the ladies' restroom with their moms. The men's bathroom usually has overflowing urinals and toilets, which means you have to walk on your tippy-toes so you aren't standing in murky pee-water.

Hoods and greasers rumble their freshly washed and waxed hotrods, choppers and cycles to the very back row of the drive-in so they can smoke, smooch, and sip their beer privately. High school teenyboppers know better than to park in the back row.

Teenyboppers act as awkward as their ages. They try to fit in somewhere between the families, which have squealing kids and the hoods and greasers as inconspicuously as possible. Hopefully, they can quietly 'neck' without being seen by a neighbor, or chided by the hoods.

Before we left, Mom and Dad told us not to wander around the drive-in by ourselves, but Celeste is very cooperative on that point once she found her boyfriend at the concession stand. She and Marianne promise not to tell on us, and we promise not to tell on them.

As soon as we are parked and set up, it is already dark and we are out of the car and on the prowl. We are quickly strolling up and down the gravel parking area between the cars looking for our friends, but we never find any. The guys are probably out playing hide-and-seek somewhere in the neighborhood.

It is a perfect summer night, and all of the families are lounging outside under the stars instead of being cooped-up inside their cars. The real Catholic families, those with lots of kids, brought blankets and aluminum lawn chairs for the kids and loungers for the parents. Chairs and blankets are set down in front of the cars or on the hoods and roofs of the cars. The largest families came very early and reserved the empty parking space next to their cars so there is plenty of space for chairs, blankets, coolers and toys. It's the family's night out and everyone came prepared for a long night of entertainment.

Trying to watch the movie and walk at the same time didn't work out too well for me. I bruised both of my shins, when I banged into the back of a Ford station wagon. I also stepped on Joey's heels twice not watching where I was going, when I saw boys and girls necking in the cars.

Teenyboppers with dates prefer to stay inside their cars no matter how hot or cold the weather got. Inside their cars, they are less conspicuous cuddling and kissing. Older boys without dates lay across the hoods of their dad's cars, and watch the chicks wearing short-shorts parade in front of their cars. All of the teenyboppers hope to get some attention, 'picked up' or collect a phone number.

The Aces are doing some field surveillance of our own. We are spying on the teenyboppers and greasers, but I wasn't sure what I was supposed to see. We strolled and gawked as much as we could without getting punched for our troubles.

Every once in a while somebody would yell, "Why don't you take a picture, it'll last longer?" or "What are you looking at you little creeps? Do you want a knuckle sandwich?"

Intimated, we'd walk a little faster and act like we quit watching them. After we trudged around the drive-in for about an hour, we stopped to empty the pea-gravel out of our Keds. That's when Joey got another one of his daring ideas.

"Let's go walk along the back row with the greasers, you guys."

"What're you crazy Joey? We'll get killed! Those guys don't want any punks hanging around them. They'll murder us."

"No it's okay. They won't hurt us. Let's go." And with that, we were trailing behind Joey trying to get him to stop, but he didn't waiver. He had his mind, and ours, set on seeing the back row. My nerves made me shiver as I stayed in the back of the pack.

By the time we arrived at the end of the back row, I was nervously talking to myself about how this was a big mistake and we were going to get killed. Joey looked very relaxed as he commanded, "Act cool Mickey."

The back row of the Airway was especially darker than the rest of the drive-in, and the hoods and greasers were so loud nobody wanted to park near them. You couldn't even hear the movie over their car radios, which were playing rock and roll and doo-wop music. We couldn't hear or see very much either.

There was a large cloud of billowing smoke floating over everyone's head because almost everybody had a lit cigarette in his or her hand. The only lights I saw were reflected off the bright silvery chrome that was on every hotrod and motorcycle parked in the back row.

If the chrome had been gold, the greasers would have been rich not just glitzy. All of the hotrods and motorcycles have chrome wheels, and the coolest looking hotrods have shiny full moon chrome hubcaps over their full chrome reverse wheels. Some also have chrome sidewinder exhaust pipes that extend along the bottoms of the cars from the motors. The ends of the pipes are either flared, low to the ground, swept up, or all of the above. The hotrods' engines are so customized and built up that the guys can't put hoods over their engines unless they cut holes in the hoods. Huge chrome carburetors, valve covers and manifolds are all exposed for easy viewing. They look powerful and beautiful. It is like being at a hotrod car show.

As we moseyed and gawked at the people and hotrods, nobody seemed to notice us or care that we are there. Nobody even looked at us much less said a word to us. Everyone was laughing, smoking cigarettes, and drinking beer. When they finished a 'butt' they'd flick the lit cigarette butt into the gravel. When someone finished a beer, they'd throw the empty bottle or can over the Airway's wire fence into a field. I especially noticed where they threw the empty bottles because I was planning to collect them for their two-cent deposits in the morning. I had seen some of the hotrods at Streak's house before. Most of the hotrods and motorcycles were painted with bright neon colors like orange, blue, red and lime green. Some of them also had flames, girlfriends' names and Goo-goo eyeballs painted on them. I didn't see Streak's motorcycle anywhere.

From the darkness, we heard a gruff voice say, "Come over here you punks!" Startled, I was ready to bolt, and then I heard the voice again. "Get over here you punks!" I was shaking.

I was about to run and scream, "Run!" when I heard a familiar laugh. It was Streak's voice, but I couldn't see him through the smoky haze, until he stepped away from the brightest, yellowest hotrod, I had ever seen.

Streak was holding a can of Falstaff beer, but he never smoked. He was dressed in his tight, black, sleeveless t-shirt, tight blue jeans, wide black belt with a silver buckle, and black motorcycle boots with silver chains. His wavy blonde hair was perfectly combed and held in place by a little dab of Brylcreem.

"What're you punks doing here? Aren't you supposed to be in bed?" he said with a smile that was as bright as his hotrod's chrome.

"No," said Joey, "Our parents know we're here. It's okay."

"Yeah, sure they do," smiled Streak, "Do they know you're walking in the back row?"

"No," said Joey, "but if they knew you were here, it'd be okay."

"Yeah sure," said Streak mocking Joey as he stepped back and pointed to the yellow hotrod, "What do you think of my new ride?"

"That's cherry Streak!" I said trying to sound a little too cool, "What kind of car is it?"

"It's a '56 Chevy Nomad," said Jimmie matter-of-factly as he surprised all of us with his knowledge of cars. "But it sure ain't stock. Look at those racing slicks on the back! That's a race car!" he yelled a little too excitedly to be cool.

"Who's your new wingman, boys?" asked Streak as he pointed to Jimmie.

"This is Jimmie," said Joey.

"Yeah," I said, way too excited. "We started a club named the Aces. We got a secret clubhouse and everything. Do you want to join Streak?"

"Maybe later Mickey. First, I want to know how Jimmie found out about the Nomad."

"My dad has a subscription to *Popular Science* and I read it."

"Cool," purred Streak as a gorgeous woman layered in colorful make-up and ratted jet-black hair slinked up behind Streak to hug him from behind. I'd never seen her before.

"Take a look at her boys," said Streak as he motioned for us to follow him.

"She's not your old girlfriend Streak." I said, thinking he wanted me to look at the girl.

"Streak doesn't mean to look at his girlfriend Mickey. He wants us to look at his Nomad," chided Joey. Everybody was laughing at me, which made me feel foolish. I followed them but I was disappointed that Streak wasn't with Lola.

I never saw a hot rod that looked as 'tough' as Streak's bright neon yellow Nomad. It stood on four black tires with raised white lettering that said *Firestone*. The back tires were really wide, completely smooth and looked a little flat—Streak told us they were racing slicks. On the very back of the car there were two small metal wheels that were extended from the frame. The metal wheels weren't touching the ground. Streak told us they were wheelie bars, so the Nomad wouldn't tip over backward when he did a wheelie.

The Nomad's huge chrome carburetor had a chrome cap with three gigantic holes the size of baseballs that looked like three wide-open mouths. Its hood had chrome locks and a large hole so the carburetor could fit through it. Streak's Nomad was a classic muscle car.

He bragged, "Look at her interior boys. It's rolled and pleated black leather. Feel it!" He let me sit in the driver's seat. You could see and hear the pride in his voice as he ran his hands lovingly over the seats.

Streak did all of the mechanical work and custom painting on his cars and motorcycles.

As we finished our tour of the Nomad, Streak said, "Why don't you boys come down to Hall Street with me tonight after the movies?"

"You know our parents won't let us Streak," said Joey sadly.

"Sneak out of your house boys, I promise it'll be a gas," winked Streak.

"You can sit next to me," cooed Streak's girlfriend in my ear as I jumped. Everyone laughed except me.

"Are you going to drag race tonight?" asked Jimmie.

"Nope. Dragging is for losers. This is a wheelie machine. I built this baby to drive a quarter-mile wheelie. It's got 700 fire-breathing horses under that hood waiting to gallop. I can't hold her back, boys," he laughed out loud as he patted the front fender of the Nomad.

"Well hello Wilbur, how are you tonight?" asked a calm friendly voice from a black silhouette with a bright flashlight. The voice sounded like Streak's best friend.

"Who's there? That's not my name," snarled Streak as he reeled around to face the silhouette. The look on Streak's face changed instantly from our friendly neighbor's smile to a look so dark and angry that I didn't recognize him.

Instantly, all of the loud music went quiet and all of the loud friendly chatter went silent as Sergeant Rogers stepped out from the shadows and confronted Streak face-to-face.

"How are you ladies and gentlemen doing tonight?" asked Sergeant Rogers just as pleasant as if he was chatting with someone after church. Then in order, he stared right through Joey, then Jimmie and finally me. I almost melted from embarrassment, but Officer Rogers was smiling the whole time.

Swallowing hard I said, "I am fine, Mister, um I mean, Sergeant Rogers. How's Robby?" I tried to sound as respectful and innocent as possible. I knew I hadn't done anything bad yet I felt really guilty.

"Well Mickey, I hope he's home with his mom. I sure don't want him hanging out at the drive-in with a bunch of hoods," dared Sergeant Rogers as he turned his stare towards Streak who had taken a step toward him. Streak stopped cold, when Sergeant Rogers showed the wooden nightstick in his right hand. I could see his holstered revolver on his thick, black leather belt.

Smiling, Officer Rogers said, "You haven't said hello Wilbur. Don't you like me?"

"*I HATE COPS!*" snarled Streak with a viciousness that dripped off each syllable.

"I heard there was a car that looked like this one," said Sergeant Rogers tapping his nightstick on the Nomad's fender, "and that the Bridgeton police were chasing it late last night on Missouri Bottom Road. Do you know anything about that Wilbur?"

"Quit hitting my Nomad. It's a shame those cops' cars weren't fast enough to catch it and give the driver a ticket," sneered Streak as he looked back at his friends for support as some of them threw their empty beer bottles over the fence and stepped closer.

"Say please Wilbur," replied Sergeant Rogers as he tapped the hood of the Nomad with his stick once again.

"Oh we'll catch him, Wilbur. Don't worry about that. Guys like him always get caught because they do stupid things," said Sergeant Rogers. "Like drinking beer at the drive-in tonight. You and your little friends know you're not supposed to drink beer here. The Airway's a family drive-in not some beer joint for you and your hooligans to hangout."

"Quit hitting my Nomad. Please. We aren't hurting anybody. Just leave us alone."

"I'm a peace officer Wilbur. I'm here to keep the peace. You and your friends are too loud, you're drinking beer, and you're throwing your beer bottles everywhere. Now, you and your friends are going to dump your beer over there in that trash can and be quiet or you have to leave the drive-in right now!" demanded Sergeant Rogers as he tapped the end of his nightstick into the palm of his other hand to the slow beat of one—two, one—two.

"You aren't taking our beer, Copper," hissed Streak.

"Then you and your friends have to leave Wilbur."

"I told you my name's not Wilbur, Copper. It's Streak."

"You're wrong. Wilbur is your God-given name. It's on your birth certificate and your arrest records. Goodbye Wilbur!" said Officer Rogers as he pointed his nightstick to the Airway's exit gate and unflinchingly stared directly into Streak's eyes.

Streak's face turned such a bright shade of red under the glare of the drive-in's lights that I thought he would explode. Abruptly, he stormed away from Sergeant Rogers who never flinched, and jumped into his Nomad. His new girlfriend stumbled on her high heels and chased after him so she wouldn't be left behind.

Before Streak slammed the Nomad's door shut, it's carburetor roared to life with deafening explosions that sounded like rolling thunder. I actually saw fire spit from the carburetor's throats as Streak floored the gas pedal time and time again, which created deafening reverberations from the Nomad's exhaust pipes. The hotter the Nomad's engine got, the louder it sounded until it sounded louder than the McDonnell Douglas jets that flew overhead breaking the sound barrier.

The Nomad's booming sounds echoing through the summer night sky was the sign for Streak's entourage to fire up their chromed engines too. The Nomad was leaving, and everyone was supposed to follow wherever it led.

Streak didn't take the shortest route to the Airway exit; instead he turned his exodus into a slow, deliberate broiling procession to save face from his run-in with Officer Rogers. The Nomad's long-drawn-out motorcade had at least 15 hotrods and just as many motorcycles buzzing around them. Each driver took up the Nomad's reverberating war cry, but the Nomad's engine was the loudest.

All of the drivers spun their tires, which spit the pea-sized gravel like bullets as they revved their engines to get their exhaust pipes rapping. Their engines were so loud nobody could hear the "Wheelers and Dealers" movie that was being broadcast through the drive-in's speakers.

The procession's thunderous explosions from the engines were so loud and lasted so long that people were climbing onto the hoods and roofs of their cars to see what was causing the noise and racket. As the Nomad slunk out of the exit many minutes later, I saw the neon yellow Nomad still belching explosions of red and yellow fire.

Fixing a stern eye on us, Sergeant Rogers said, "I better never see you boys hanging out with Wilbur again or I'll tell your parents. Do you hear me?"

"Yes sir," we sang in chorus.

"Now let's get you boys back where you belong," said Sergeant Rogers as he pushed us in our backs to get us moving. In a matter of minutes, he had us sitting in front of the Rambler on our blankets, eating our popcorn and drinking ice-cold lemonade. Celeste and Marianne were glum because Sergeant Rogers sent their boyfriends back to their own car saying, "I don't want anyone to get into any trouble on my watch!"

As we waited for *It's A Mad, Mad, Mad World* to start, I tried to calculate how much deposit money I'd collect tomorrow from all of those beer bottles thrown over the drive-in's fence. I couldn't get Sergeant Rogers out of my mind. He never looked scared of Streak—not one second.

Chapter 14

The Last Inning of Our Summer

dults always say, "It doesn't matter if you win or lose, it's how you play the game," but it is the bottom of the last inning of our summer and winning is all that matters to any of us guys.

The Suzie's are winning eight runs to six, but the V.F.W. Rebels are up to bat and it's the top of their batting order. Their best player, Gus McGloat, is their clean up hitter, and he is batting fourth this inning. Gus is the best hitter in our league.

This isn't one of our regularly scheduled league games. It's a grudge match between the Rebels and the Suzies. We are playing for pride. Our regular season games are over and our two teams ended up tied for first place in our league.

Our regular baseball season didn't start out being very much fun, but we're playing like our old selves now.

There aren't any parents or coaches at this game. Just players. Each team brought its nine best players to this game. The only adult is Mr. Solomon. He is our neighborhood mailman, and he doesn't have any kids. He's using his lunch break to umpire our game. Everybody likes Mr. Solomon and none of us argue with his calls. The losing team has to help him finish his mail route after the game.

The Suzies never completely shook the spectacle of our new Suzie's Tomatoes uniforms. Everybody made fun of us to our faces and behind our backs. Heck, even our parents, brothers, and sisters teased us.

Today is different. We are playing in our blue jeans and t-shirts again, and each Suzie is wearing his favorite ball cap. Mine is the Cardinals, with Stan Musical's card stuck in the headband. The Rebels are playing in their official team uniforms.

Neither team has been able to dominate the game. The score has been tied at the end of each inning. It's the top of the ninth inning and we have a two run lead, after I coaxed a walk and Paul hit a double driving me to third. Ed, our first baseman, hit a sacrifice fly ball almost to Ashby Road that drove in Paul and me.

The Rebels' first batter struck out in the bottom of the ninth inning. Our pitcher, Denny, who is the best pitcher in our league, threw him a change-up pitch, after he fouled off four consecutive fastballs for the strikeout. It is our team's habit of calling a huddle with all of the infielders after a tough out, so I called time out and walked out to the mound to give Denny a rest and check our signals.

"Holy cow, we got lucky there," exhaled Ed as he wiped the sweat off his forehead with the back of his hand.

Taking off my mask, I said, "It wasn't luck. It was a great pitch Ed. Great pitch, Denny!" I said trying to build his confidence and give Ed my nastiest look.

Ed just ignored me, "I hope Gus doesn't bat this inning, he's gotten a hit every time he's been to the plate today."

"I'm not scared of Gus what's-his-name," crowed Denny, "he's just been lucky today that's all."

"That's right Denny, he's been lucky," I echoed, hoping that Gus didn't get another bat this game either. Secretly, we all did, and Denny probably did too.

"Well you better pray Gus doesn't get another bat," chided Ed smugly.

"Let's go boys, my lunch break was over an hour ago," Mr. Solomon urged, prodding us along by clapping his hands.

"Okay guys, remember, the out is at first and use two hands Eddie," I ordered smacking my mitt for emphasis. As everyone returned to his position, I wiped the dust off the ball and handed it to Denny.

"Let's get this out Denny!" I said looking him straight in the eyes. He nodded and pulled his cap down tighter on his head.

After I hustled back to the plate, I turned to face my players, pointed my right index to heaven and yelled, "One out, and the second one's at the plate!" I chuckled as I pulled my mask over my face and crouched.

The second batter was the Rebel coach's son, Jack Junior. His nickname was J.J. and he was as cocky as he was good. He made me a little nervous so I gave him some chatter at the plate.

"I really want you guys to win J.J. so just swing, when I tell you to swing and you'll get a hit. I promise."

"Shut-up Mickey." J.J. smirked as he spit and knocked the dust out of the treads of his well-worn Keds with the tip of his bat.

"Okay," I sighed, acting like my feelings were hurt, "all I'm trying to do is help."

"Yeah, right, Mickey," he scoffed, "If you want to help put on some deodorant. You have B.O. so bad you're stinking up the whole field, you dustball."

It was obvious J.J. wanted to make this personal when he insulted my hygiene. Everybody knew the catcher was the dirtiest player on a team. That's why I like to play catcher. Everybody else on the team looked the same after most games. They had a few sweat stains and some dust on their hips if they slid into a base. Heck some of the guys practice sliding just to get dirty, but I never have to act like I am dirty. I am the hardest working guy on the team and I am proud of the fact that I am the dirtiest player on the field too.

The catcher is always the sweatiest and dirtiest player on any team. His face is dirty where the mask rubs against his cheeks, and his dirt stained chest and legs are obvious markers where his sweaty chest protector and shin guards have been strapped on the whole game. Catchers also get to wear their hats backwards whenever they want. It's our off-the-field badge of honor.

"You got it J.J." I smiled deciding to insult him one better. After a moment's thought, I decided against insulting his mother and decided to insult him by using his girlfriend Nancy.

"Better yet J.J., I'll borrow some of Nancy's best perfume, when I see her after the game. She's not going to want to hang out with you, after you lose to a bunch of guys named Suzie," I chided, as I crouched on my toes on the inside corner of the plate.

J.J. sneered back at me as he took a couple of practice swings and stared a hole through Denny, who was looking hot and tired.

Instead of an inside, low fastball, Denny's first pitch was a fastball right down the middle of the plate waist high. Mistakenly, I said, "Swing!" and J.J. launched a line drive between our left and center fielders. As the outfielders scrambled to catch up to the ball and throw to our shortstop, Kevin, J.J. slid into second base for an easy double. That was one of the main things I didn't like about J.J., he was a 'show boater.'

As he stood on second base and dusted off his pants and shirt, we all knew he really didn't have to slide. There was no play at the base. J.J. did it for show. From second base, he yelled to me, "Thanks for telling me to swing, Mickey! You were right!"

Denny gave me a dirty-look as did most of the other Suzies. He was a fun loving lanky guy, who didn't usually say much, when he was pitching, but he was motioning me out to the mound. I shuffled out to the mound kicking up a path of dust as I went.

"Don't say anything to nobody Mickey," Denny said looking hurt at the thought that I'd betray him.

"Sorry," I whispered as I hustled back to the plate and pulled the mask over my dirt-stained face and crouched behind the plate.

There was one out, and one guy on base. Drew was at the plate, and Gus was taking practice swings on deck. We needed an out badly—right now.

Drew had been our team's second baseman before he double-crossed us and left to play with the Rebels two years ago. His high treason had caused bad blood. Since his defection, he had never had a very good game against us—luckily.

"Will you tell me when to swing too, Mickey?" laughed Drew as he dug into the left side of the batter's box.

"Sure Drew, I'll do anything for a friend," I countered, intimating that he wasn't my friend anymore and never would be.

We all knew that since J.J. got on base, Gus was going to bat this inning unless we got a double play somehow. If Drew got on base too, then Gus, the most fearsome homerun hitter in our league would be the winning run when he got to the plate.

Suddenly, I remembered Coach Starr always had Drew bunt in situations like this because he was the best bunter and a fast runner too. He wasn't as fast as me, but he was as fast as Dave. Since he didn't have any hits yet this game, I knew Drew was feeling the pressure to get on base.

"Bunt!" I yelled loudly "Bunt!" All of the infielders shook their heads in agreement and cheated in two steps closer to home plate. All that is except Ed, who was too slow to get back to first base. It was up to Denny or me to pick up the bunt down the first base line and throw Drew out at first base and hold J.J. at second base.

Nervously, Denny threw his first pitch high and outside, it was a ball. His second pitch was barely outside and missed being a strike even though I had quickly pulled it back over the plate. Mr. Solomon was a good ump and hard to fool.

At two balls and no strikes, Denny had to throw a strike. Drew knew it and I watched him smile as he got ready with a couple of light swings trying to fake us out. As Denny's pitch sped home, Drew shifted his weight, squared around at the plate, moved his right hand up the barrel of the bat, and got ready to bunt. I guessed wrong and was caught off balance. Drew bunted down the third base line not the first base line and it was up to Mike to make the play.

Mike charged in hard from third base to grab the sputtering baseball with his bare hand. Kevin ran from short to cover third base. As Mike held the ball near his right ear, he stared at J.J. who had a big lead off second base, and dared him to run to third. Mike waited just a half second too long before he threw to Ed at first base. Drew was safe and J.J. was still on second base.

One out. Base runners on second and first, and Gus, the winning run, was at the plate. Things didn't look too good and they felt even worse. Our whole season rested on getting the next batter out and Gus McGloat was their best hitter.

It was time for the Suzies to huddle at the mound, so I looked at Mr. Solomon imploringly, who sighed resignedly, raised my mitt into the air and yelled "Time out!" We jogged to the mound for what would probably be our last huddle of the season.

"Any ideas?" I asked the guys.

"Yeah, walk Gus," said Ed, "load the bases for a force-out anywhere."

"Sounds good to me," said Bob and Mike shook his head in agreement.

"What do you think Denny?" I asked hopefully. Denny never walked anybody willingly, especially Gus, and especially in this situation.

"I ain't walking that guy," said Denny. "If *YOU* want to walk Gus, get another pitcher. I ain't chicken of Gus."

"Denny, Gus's killing us," he's already hit a home run, a double and single. You have to walk him," pleaded Ed.

"Not me, I ain't winning that way," said Denny stoically. "You walk him Ed, and I'll play first," countered Denny as he started towards first base.

"Wait Denny," I said, taking charge. "You're our pitcher. We want you pitching to Gus. Come on guys, let's stick together," I pleaded as I pounded my fist into my mitt for emphasis, "We need two outs—*right now*!"

I declared as I pounded my mitt again. Then I handed the game ball back to Denny after I wiped the dust off it.

"Come on Denny, throw strikes so we can win this thing—*right now*!" I demanded.

Denny had returned to the mound with a slight smile on his face. I admired that he was as cool as a cucumber. He acted like he had everything under control.

That is the way pitchers have to think. The world might be falling apart and they have to think everything is going to be fine. To Denny, it was a picnic in the park. It didn't matter one bit that the guy standing in the batter's box had been smashing his pitches all day long and had already driven in most of their team's runs. Denny believed he was going to win the battle with Gus at the plate this time.

I wasn't as confident as Denny. I was praying like a sinner at St. Peter's gate. I had been praying a lot faster than Denny had been pitching all day, and it was time to say as many Hail Mary's as I could before I crossed home plate. Although I prayed quietly, I made the sign of the cross as I crouched into position. Gus saw me out of the corner of his eye.

I wasn't sure if God would respond to my prayers for help but I figured my prayers couldn't hurt. I believe God loves me and is always trying to teach me important lessons.

The challenge is knowing what God thinks is the best lesson for me to learn. Today I'm not sure.

Does He want to teach me humility and how to be a good loser? Or, is He trying to teach that lesson to Gus and give me a little heaven on earth by letting the Suzies win? That's the thing about God. You never know for sure what He's thinking. You just have to believe it's going to be OK in the end.

Pulled from my moment of reverie, I heard Gus smugly hiss, "You better pray Mickey because I'm going to smash this ball so far your outfielders aren't ever going to find it."

Faking confidence, I jibed, "I'm not praying for us Gus. I'm praying for you. I don't want you feeling too bad after you make an out." I pounded my mitt, got set, and gave Denny a low target on the inside part of the plate.

"I don't need any prayers," growled Gus, "All I need is my trusty Joe DiMaggio, here," as he waved his bat over his head. Gus batted with a 32-inch, blonde wood Joe DiMaggio bat that had been his dad's. He only used it for important games like this one. He treated the bat like it was made of solid gold. He even had his mom make a case for it out of an old towel that matched the color of his uniform.

Denny took his time and used his extra long double-pump windup. Then, he hit my mitt with his best fastball of the day. Gus swung and missed and Mr. Solomon yelled, *"Steerriikke one!"*

"Thanks for the breeze, Gus," I said mockingly, I've never been this hot before. Just keep fanning away," I laughed.

Gus didn't answer me. He was too good of a ball player to lose his concentration and cool for a smart-alecky comment from me. Instead, Gus stepped out of the batter's box, took a slow practice swing, and stepped back into the batter's box. Gingerly, he tapped the outside corner of the plate and tightened his grip around his Joe DiMaggio. I could see DiMaggio's autograph printed on the bat's barrel.

My next target for Denny was high and inside. Gus was a sucker for high pitches, but if you didn't put them inside, he would hit them across Ashby Road and they wouldn't stop rolling until they hit the St. Ann golf course fence.

Denny hit my target with another sizzling fastball as Gus swung and missed again, Mr. Solomon yelled, *"Steerriikke two!"* Then, Mr. Solomon raised his fists into the air so everyone could see that there were no balls and two strikes on Gus.

I felt giddy I was so excited. "You're too good to me Gus. You know I'm boiling in all this gear and your swings are keeping me as cool as a *Popsicle*. Do you want that prayer now?" I wisecracked.

"Naw, me and Mr. DiMaggio are doing just fine Mickey," said Gus, as he stepped out of the batter's box and took another slow practice swing. Then, he stepped back into the batter's box, and like always touched the outside corner of the plate with his DiMaggio and got ready. Denny's next pitch was right on target—low and outside. Unfortunately, Gus didn't take our bait.

"Ball," yelled Mr. Solomon.

Denny had been our best pitcher all year and he was pitching great. All of his pitches had extra zip and he didn't look tired anymore. He was focused and pitching better than he had pitched all day. His last three pitches hit my targets without me having to move my mitt an inch, but Gus was a tough customer, and we needed two more outs to win the game.

After three fastballs, the next pitch I signaled for was a change-up but Denny shook me off. Then I signaled for a fastball low and inside but Denny shook me off again. Finally, it hit me. Denny wanted to throw his curve ball. His dad had taught him how to throw a curve during the summer. It wasn't his best pitch but he loved it. Sometimes his curve was too slow and it didn't curve at all. It just floated right down the middle of the plate. So, I tried signaling for another high fastball inside but Denny shook me off for the third time. Frustrated, I signaled Denny for a curveball, which he accepted with a big smile as he started his double-pump windup.

Gus's facial expression didn't change one iota as he pounced on Denny's curve ball. The pitch was perfect but Gus connected big time with his DiMaggio.

All I heard was "Caaa-Raaackkkkk" as Gus launched Denny's curveball so furiously that everybody just stood still staring at it in disbelief. The baseball's speed and trajectory looked like a McDonnell-Douglas jet taking off at Lambert Airport. We were all whomper-jawed— even Denny.

Luckily, Gus, J.J. and Drew momentarily stood still watching and admiring it too. Everybody was standing in awe but Dave and Kevin. They started chasing Gus's fly ball like it was a hundred-dollar bill. By the time Gus started his cocky homerun stroll around the bases, Dave was crossing Ashby Road to retrieve the ball as it came to rest against the golf course fence. Kevin had run from shortstop until he was standing in deep right-centerfield waiting for Dave's throw.

That's when all of the base runners realized it might be a close play and started sprinting as fast as they could. Seeing Dave and Kevin hustle made the rest of the Suzies take heart and get into motion. Mike ran to cover third base and Rusty ran from second to short-center for Kevin's relay throw. Denny covered second base and Ed trudged towards home, which I was blocking, to back me up. Still, with no baseball in sight, J.J. stepped on home plate and cut our lead to one run.

Dave's perfect line-drive throw got to Kevin at the same time Drew stepped on third base. This was the kind of play Kevin dreamed about every day of his life.

Kevin is our best fielder and he can play almost every position on the team as good as the guy playing it. He loves to play shortstop best and practices more than any other guy.

He goes to the Kroger store and draws different sized squares and circles on the brick wall at different heights and throws hundreds of rubber balls to improve his aim and velocity everyday—rain or shine. He loves baseball more than anybody even Stan Musial. He collects the players' cards and their plastic statues. He knows every player and every team and all of their statistics. He wants to be a professional ball player and we all believe he will someday.

Everything went into slow motion for me as Kevin caught Dave's throw over his right shoulder as he ran towards home plate. After taking a couple of giant running crow-hops that ended as a jump into the air

Kevin threw a line drive from the outfield so low and so fast that Rusty and Denny had to belly flop to the ground so they wouldn't get hit with it as it went whistling overhead. Even Gus was worried about getting hit so he slowed down as he was heading for second base.

There was going to be a play at the plate, so I was blocking the third base line just like Coach Starr had taught me. I had thrown my mask out of the way and held my mitt knee high because Kevin's one-bounce throw was a perfect peg to the plate. Mr. Solomon was in position next to home plate on the first base line to make the call as Drew started his hard slide to home plate. The ball made a loud THUD as it hit my mitt, which was blocking the plate, a quarter-of-a-second before Drew's foot tried to kick the ball out of my mitt.

I had the ball wrapped with both hands as Mr. Solomon signaled a fist into the air and yelled, *"YOU'RE OUT!"*

That's when I heard Mike screaming, "Third base, Mickey—get him at third!" Frantically, I looked up at Mike straddling third base blocking Gus's path to the bag. As I pulled the ball from my mitt to my ear, Gus charged hard. He was getting ready to slide into third. I knew that I could throw Gus out if my throw landed in Mike's glove, which was lying in front of third base. It did.

As the dust cloud cleared from Gus's slide, Mr. Solomon, who had run from home towards third yelled, *"YOU'RE OUT!"* and signaled a fist with his right hand into the air. Mike's glove had kept Gus's right foot from touching third base.

The Suzies went wild. We met at the mound and jumped on each other, rolled on the ground, knocked each other down, threw dust at each other and threw our gloves and hats into the air yipping and yelling so loud we got hoarse. The Rebels were as quiet as if they were in church. They didn't make a sound as Mr. Solomon walked over to their dugout and congratulated them on how well they played.

After the Suzies saw Mr. Solomon, we huddled together and gave the same cheer Coach Starr made us give for every team we played after every game, win or lose.

"Two-four-six, eight, who do we appreciate? The Rebels!" and then we wildly threw our hats and gloves into the air again. Then we gave another loud cheer for Mr. Solomon before we started collecting our stuff so everyone could help him deliver the mail. We were feeling sky high.

As I jogged back towards home plate to get my facemask and cap, I met with Gus, who was looking down at his broken Joe DiMaggio bat. There were tears on his cheek as he picked up his cracked bat and looked at it. I didn't say anything except, "Great hit Gus!" and I meant it.

CPSIA information can be obtained
at www.ICGtesting.com
Printed in the USA
LVHW051155141220
674127LV00034B/1209